ADVANCED PRAISE FOR
WHERE POP STARS GO TO DIE

"David Washburn's 'Where Pop Stars Go To Die' poses the question 'What if your favorite pop star became a final girl?' and answers with a blood-spattered bang. Pink horror approved fun!"
—Wendy Dalrymple, author of BIRTHDAY PARTY DEMON and CREDENZA—

"Where Pop Stars Go to Die is what happens when the glitz of musical fame meets the grit of true horror. This book hit all the right notes: combining innovative kills and visceral terror with the absolute fever dream that is pop star culture. The unique combination of narrative devices keeps the world feeling realistic and immersive; I love it when authors take the risk and blend these somewhat experimental styles. It really paid off for Washburn's novel and was incredibly effective. Gory, glamorous, and impossible to put down."
—Megan Stockton, author of BLUEJAY—

"Washburn's writing shines in this gruesomely wicked novel."
—Amy Tackett, author of THE GALA and SECRET SANTA—

"Washburn delivers a tense and unsettling rollercoaster ride that showcases a talent for 'finger on the pulse' modern horror."
—A.D. Jones, author of LITTLE HORN—

"I didn't just read this. I felt it. This book is a brutal, fast-paced ride that's as addictive as it is unputdownable. Think Squid Game or Hunger Games colliding with pop culture icons like Taylor Swift and Britney Spears, then throw in a deadly dose of dark art and twisted survival."

—Arti Manani, author of 'TIL DEATH DO US PART and THE NEIGHBOUR—

"Where Pop Stars Go to Die is a gripping, heart pounding story about resilience, fame, and the fight to take back control."

—Kirsten Noelle Craig, author of THE CURSE OF MEDUSA—

"Highly original. An exhilarating thrill ride full of tension, action, and plenty of gore. A definite must-read! David Washburn's writing just gets better and better!"

—Jason A. Jones, author of STARVING ALICE and THE PUMP-KIN PIE MAN—

"This book chews up fame, spits out the bones, and dares you to keep watching. Washburn delivers a fever dream of captivity, spectacle, and survival that left me gutted."

—Mo Medusa, author of FEEDING LUCY—

"Washburn expertly weaves a tale of psychological horror filled with visceral and physical danger, raising the stakes at every turn."

—Danielle Morris, author of BIRDS OF A FEATHER and IN ALL MY DREAMS—

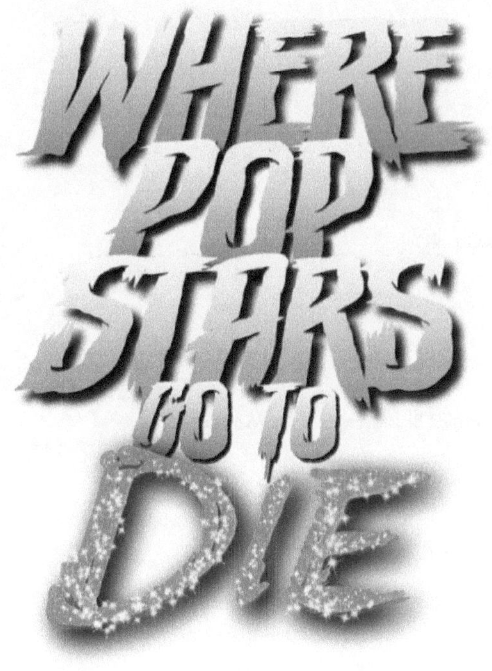

DAVID WASHBURN

Where Pop Stars Go to Die

© 2025 by David Washburn

All Rights Reserved

Cover Design by Fabled Beast Design | A.A. Medina

Interior Design by Joey Powell

Proofread & Edited by Kaylynn Wurzelbacher

Published by Burn Ward Publishing

www.WASHBURNWRITES.com

Instagram & Threads: @WashburnWrites

Email: DavidWritesStories@gmail.com

Between 16,000 and 20,000 people go missing in the Netherlands
each year.

Most missing persons are eventually found.

. . . Most.

1

Lights flash so bright I can hardly see. The beams sting my skin and any brief moment I find to stand still and catch my breath, I feel it against the sweat on my face. I'm just trying to keep smiling. If I weren't so used to it by now I might complain, but those lights are what pay the bills, or one might even say . . . keep the lights on. The illumination is so alluring, like God revealing Himself just before the pyro goes off.

Boom!

Right on cue as I take calculated steps across the catwalk. Steps I've rehearsed for months before doing the same mechanical movements multiple nights a week for the last year and a half. Mostly in the United States . . . and now internationally. Twelve steps ahead as my hips sway in an exaggerated showcase of confidence and strength. All of the eyes crawl across my body just before the next one.

Boom! There it is!

Those eyes, I feel every single night, and sometimes I can't tell if those are the chills I get when the tens of thousands of screaming Foxies are singing along to the songs I've written and tediously perfected on this stage, or if it's how nervous I still feel every show despite the fact that I've been doing this since I was thirteen. Those nerves never go away apparently, but I've come to learn how to use them. I get nervous before doing anything that matters and this is the life I always dreamed of—and this is what matters most.

Boom!

Standing at the edge of the stage, I wait for the stage lights to hit the floor so I know my mark. The music is never an issue, but there's always a chance that unpredictability shows its face and someone's timing is off. The production is at another level compared to where we started over fifteen years ago.

I hit my mark.

I freeze as the stadium lights go out and my band lets the music fade. First the drums end with a fill as the crowd screams, filling the void space of percussion in the song. The bass continues to hum even though my bassist stopped strumming. The guitar growls through the amps along with the atmospheric synths that come from the keyboard like a harmonic hangover. The spotlight on the floor makes me look like a silhouette.

A superstar.

A million bucks.

My final outfit of the night that I happen to catch a glance of on the Jumbotron in my peripheral makes me feel like a bedazzled supermodel. A tight soft pink and powder blue bodysuit, equipped with an unhealthy amount of glitter to satisfy my inner child. With a massive team behind this operation, I'm able to look like a superhero each and every night.

The buzz of so many adoring fans, my little Foxies . . . it's what I do this for. Every screaming little girl, teenager, young woman, and even some husbands that were dragged along, all of their faces are swallowed by the night in the stadium, but their voices make their presence well known. That buzz becomes screaming as I stand here in the light with my hip cocked, striking a dramatic pose as I fight back a smile and catch my breath. Every person in attendance is wearing a bracelet that lights up to the music, and as pro-grammed for this part of the show, their wrists light up with a bright white light and all of the hands waving in the air look like fireflies all around me. The moment is picture perfect.

Wait for it.

Adrenaline keeps me shaking even when discipline keeps me still as I . . . *wait for it.*

The crowd intensifies. Anticipation flutters in the dark after hours of a high energy performance singing all of their favorite songs. The air is alive, you can feel it crawling along your skin. This crowd, and many of the ones before tonight maintain this level of excitement and keep me engaged. Is it cliche to say that I'm grateful? Maybe, but that doesn't mean it's not true.

Wait for it.

My heart is the only thing beating in my ears right now. Each breath is bigger than the last as I can't resist smiling at the people here to sing along to all of their favorite songs. This international tour embodies almost two decades of my passion and hard work. This is me giving it back to my fans.

Wait for it.

My chest rises and falls and I concentrate on the love pouring sonically toward the stage. Toward the spotlight. My lips stretch across my face showing a toothy smile that makes my eyes squint like a child. My cheeks ache at this involuntary expression as I raise the microphone to my mouth with the same confidence as a soldier raising a weapon in battle. The fans scream louder somehow as they see me moving.

Wait for it.

. . .

Boom!

The pyro explodes and I feel the heat from it dry the sweat on the back of my neck and exposed shoulders. The crowd roars with thousands of small voices being anything but small tonight as the music hits and I finish the lyrics to the final chorus with choreographed and dramatic dance. My dancers march to the front of the stage as they split into two lines and I walk between them in the opposite direction while singing, just like every other show so far.

When I reach the end of the line of dancers, the two gentlemen at the rear drop to a knee, and I tap each of their heads, jerk my head with a laugh, and I raise my leg and slam it down on time with the crashing cymbals. The dancers jump up with hands on my waist as they raise me in the air and suddenly I'm like a cheerleader. This used to scare me, but each night it becomes more and more business as usual. I'm spun around by my dancers, and sat down with the others in a line at my sides, and me in the middle with my arms spread as wide as the smile on my face.

Cannons fire, sending confetti onto the stage and into the crowds, so much that it blocks out the lights and makes everyone look like television static among the tens of thousands screaming for this night to never end.

"I love you, Dublin!" I scream into the mic. The drums rumble as the hi hats sizzle. "Thank you!"

The crowd rattles the frame to Aviva Stadium with their voices.

"Give it up for the band, who played every note you danced to tonight!" I gesture to each band member as they stand and wave, taking in the adoration for this moment. The drummer taps on the cymbals to create magical sound before standing to wave.

"Give it up for my beautiful and talented dancers!"

The crowd goes insane as the dancers all take a step forward in unison to take a bow, just like every other night. I stand here clapping with a smile that I couldn't fight even if I wanted to. This energy is infectious and I'm too far gone. My dancers are incredible and we've worked so hard to make this production what it is. They deserve every bit of praise because with them on my team, I never feel alone out here. At first, the stage used to feel so big, and I felt so alone. But as my popularity has grown, so have the stages, and my team shares that space to help make me not feel so isolated under the massive lights and happy faces.

"And give it up for yourselves!" The crowd goes nuts with a giant roar. "Thank you, thank you, *thank you* so much for welcoming us to your home." I take in the roaring cheers from the seats. "You've shown us so much love and we're happy to give it right back! I wish I could stay and meet every single one of your beautiful faces." The smile I wear hurts my cheeks as I look out to the fans screaming one final passionate cheer. I see young girls bouncing up and down and crying. People wiping their eyes, some even grown women. "I promise I'll come back soon, Ireland! We love you!" I shout as I wave goodbye and blow kisses. The stage lights dim and I walk among my dancers in a group as we all head behind the curtain to begin the aftershow festivities.

"Miss Fox," one of the production assistants says as she taps my shoulder.

I take a big swig of water and meet her eyes. "Yes?"

She walks alongside me, scrolling through an agenda on her tablet. "Great show, Miss Fox."

"Phoebe is fine," I tell her.

She stumbles at the casual way I ask to be addressed. "Um, Phoebe . . . so, you have a few guests on the unlisted VIP list waiting to meet you right now."

"Do you know who they are?"

She scrolls a bit on the tablet the other way as we keep walking. "Looks like a few local soccer players, some magazine and producer types, and a few Make-a-Wish kids. Is that okay?"

"Yeah, yes," I say, still trying to gather myself after coming off the stage. "Give me a little bit to get out of this outfit. Let's say twenty minutes."

"That'll work Miss F . . . Phoebe," she says with a smile as she pivots off into another direction, giving orders into her headset.

"See ya in a bit."

Dancers and bandmates all disperse through the back area. Some rush to catering, others to clean themselves up. I get to my dressing room and as I open the door, I see Ashton Craig sitting there, waiting on me.

2

"Hey there, Pheebs," he says as he stands.

"Hey, Ash," I say, embarrassed that the perspiration from the show is soaking through my clothes as his arms pull me close and swallow me into his chest. Thankfully, he doesn't seem to mind.

My stylist and makeup artist are both waiting to dress me down and bring me back to Earth. Normally I'll step out of my outfit and let my stylist look over it while I'm having makeup scrubbed off my face like some sort of clown. "Could you just give us a few minutes?"

"Sure, Phoebe," one of them says as they both make their way out.

The door closes behind them and I take a big inhale and soak up his scent. Cedarwood and something minty . . . something clean.

"You were incredible out there," he says with his deep voice, holding me close in his tight embrace.

"Thanks," I say, pulling back enough to look him in the eye. "Thanks for coming. It really means a lot that you would come all this way." He leans toward me and our lips lock. My arms are around his shoulders and neck for only a second before my hands are on his face, and his on my waist.

"Of course," he responds, pulling away from my lips. "I couldn't miss it." More pecks on the lips, "That crowd was insane when you came out. Like, really . . . wow!"

I pull away from his lips, leaving only a breath between us. "They're like that every night, no matter the country."

He lets me go and has a look at me. His eyes are all over my body and I tingle from the spilled-over adrenaline and his thoughts behind that look. "Well, I suppose there's a reason you're performing in stadiums, I guess it's to be expected."

With my arms spread wide and a picture-ready smile I do a runway spin for Ashton. "Well, what do ya think?"

His head nods and his smirk pulls to one side of his face as he eyes me up and down. "Well . . . you certainly pull off superhero cosplay quite well."

The laugh escapes my chest and I strike the classic hero pose with the wide-foot stance and closed fists on my waist to compliment a stoic look. "I guess I need to work a cape into my outfit now, huh?"

Ashton closes in once more with his hands on my hips and us kissing. "As long as you promise to keep it on with me . . . during a more . . . private show."

"Mmmm," I say, in more of a moan against his lips.

One of my favorite things about Ashton is how safe he feels to me. How relaxed I am with him. How we can be goofy and silly together without fear of what others think. It's the same feeling when I'd have a crush on boys as a teenager. He feels like home to me. We kiss for only a minute, but ugh, I want to do so much more. Making time to see him has been a challenge on this tour. I just try to keep in mind that there will be plenty of time later. "Listen, I don't mean to be that girl, but I have to get out of this outfit and clean up," I say with a sour tone.

I see the disappointment in his face, even behind a laugh. "I understand . . . you're a busy woman, I get it."

I go over to the vanity and have a seat and study my face in the mirror. The show lights glow above making my face look stunning, but almost *too well* lit. The room is pretty typical from most green rooms or backstage private lounge areas. A small table sits against one wall with a spread of snacks—healthy and sugary ones—and a mini fridge underneath stocked with soda, water, energy drinks, and I'm sure if I asked for it, any alcohol I might desire. A pair of modern, low-sitting couches sit across from one another with a small glass-top table offering magazines and books. Each magazine having me on the cover, and if not me, at least a mention of me in the headline. Hard to not think that was by design with the people hosting the 'Through the Years' Tour. I can't think of a time I've ever had that sort of leisure in this setting to flip through a book or magazine, but it's a nice touch.

I start grabbing makeup wipes to take off all of the glitter and makeup caked up on my face. I figure I can give my assistants a headstart while I chat and keep them waiting. "I'm super happy to see you, I'm always happy to see you, you know that. It's just that I have some obligations right now to make appearances and meet people."

He stands behind me with his rough hands on my shoulders and neck. The massaging causes my eyes to close involuntarily and I just want to fall under his spell *so* badly right now. I fight to pry open my eyes and not get too comfortable. I see him in the mirror, looking into my eyes in the reflection.

"That's okay, Pheebs . . . you give your everything to your legion of supporters for now," he leans down, breathing onto my neck. "But after this tour, you belong to me."

My skin raises and I feel my body responding in all the right ways. I catch a glimpse of the stupid smile plastered on my face in the mirror, and I can't help but to blush and somehow feel embarrassed. I sing and dance in front of a hundred-thousand people every night, yet this guy can still make me blush in private. I stand up, starting to wipe my face while I look in the mirror closely. "I need to get out of this bodysuit already," I say, offering only an awkward laugh. "So you've got to fly back home? You sure you can't fly with me to Amsterdam?"

Ashton paces slowly from wall to wall. "I'm afraid not, boss is on me to show my face in the office and I told him I'd be there after this show."

"Duh, of course . . . you have your own work." Ashton Craig, hot shot entertainment writer and music journalist.

I ball up a wipe and toss it into the waste bin at my feet. I turn to him and his eyes meet mine, "I'll hurry back and try to catch you in Italy," he kisses me. I breathe heavy through my nose, taking in more of his intoxicating scent that reminds my body how it felt only a moment ago. "Maybe Germany," he whispers, pulling away.

"Well hurry back, I can't wait to sing for you."

"Among the sold out stadium full of your minions," he snickers. "Well, don't I feel special."

"Don't call them minions," I say, hitting him as I laugh.

"I'm sorry, I'm sorry," he says, raising his hands in surrender as he backs away. "I can't stop thinking about them as minions since I saw that meme."

I kiss him one last time, deep and passionate, knowing that I'm going to only want more when he turns to leave. "Go on, get out of here," I say as I playfully push him away with a smile.

"I'll let you know when I touch down."

"Be careful."

"You too."

He leaves my dressing room and I begin to peel off my bodysuit. Ashton surprised me and killed more time than I would have liked, but selfishly, I know I can lean on the fact that this show doesn't move without me. I don't want to hold everyone up though. I wipe myself off and change into black jeans and a white t-shirt.

There is a knock at the door. "Miss Fox?"

I'll never get used to the Miss Fox thing. "It's Phoebe," I shout back. "One second."

I gather my things and toss on a black ball cap, not to hide that it's me, but maybe to hide this mess of hair. The hair that I literally gave no attention to when I changed out of my stage outfit. I open the door and my assistant is waiting there for me, along with the stylist and makeup artist and two of my body guards, Jack and Aaron. Jack is the older, more grizzled guy. Bald head and built like a powerlifter while he stands there stroking his well-groomed—but too long—beard. And then Aaron, dark hair and brown eyes, clean shaved and in phenomenal shape with an extensive military background. The two men have been my protection for the better part of a decade now, in addition to Harry and the new guy, Scott. We have a close relationship nowadays and they feel more like friends than employees, but I make sure they're taken care of and happy since they deal with a lot of nonsense to keep me safe.

"Miss Fox," my assistant starts. "Joshua Callahan and Roederick Dunne are waiting for you, along with a few other teammates."

"Hi guys," I say to Jack and Aaron.

"Phoebe," Aaron nods.

Jack nods in silence.

"These are soccer players?" I ask, turning back to my assistant. We walk and talk and as her and I lead the charge, Jack and Aaron tail us.

"Yes. Also, the owner is there as well, along with some of his executive team and stadium management. They had one of the suites tonight watching your performance."

"Awesome," I say. Jack walks ahead of us, being an excellent lookout as we peruse the complex. "And you mentioned some kids, right?"

"That's right. I've already got them set up. Their families are there and don't seem to mind waiting. Everyone is excited."

"I'm sure they're excited. I'll try to be quick."

"Harry, this is Jack, ya got a copy?" Jack says into his earpiece as we turn down a corridor decorated with large framed artwork of soccer players on one side and gorgeous landmark paintings on the other.

"The fox is out of the foxhole and enroute. Are we clear to proceed?" Jack asks. I always found it cute how serious he takes this job. Not that I don't want him to, I mean, that's what I pay him for. But after seeing him unwind and show his fun side over the years, this tough and serious exterior is almost ironic.

He stops us. Aaron is behind us. "What's the word?"

"Waiting for confirmation," Jack answers. "Standing by."

"A few of the dancers and the band are already in there," my assistant says.

"Copy that," Jack says. "Alright, we're goin' in," he says, waving us to follow. Scott stands at the suite, holding the door open. Scott is the youngest of the bunch, dark hair kept short and combed over at all times like it's always wet. A suave look that goes with his blue eyes and disarming smile. We all join the party inside.

"Miss Fox!" an older gentleman calls out with his arms spread wide. I don't bother correcting him, it's a losing battle to keep correcting everyone about my name, and I'm honestly exhausted and just ready to hop on the jet and sleep.

Sleep . . . the elusive cure-all.

I notice at least a dozen people in the suite standing around, some with bottles in their hand. They all notice me and suddenly I feel like a zoo animal. I don't mind meet and greets, and I don't mind being on stage and everyone watching me do my thing, but something about rich and powerful men I find unsettling. I put on my trademark Phoebe Fox smile and charm though, and spend ten minutes shaking hands, hugging, and chatting with people. We take a lot of photos and thankfully it isn't as bad as my anxiety convinced me it would be.

3

I say my goodbyes and my assistant ushers me along and I am out of there. As we head out, Jack is back in front, Aaron at the rear, and Harry, the red-haired teddy bear—whose muscles are threatening to burst from his polo—has joined the flank. It's not a far walk before we approach the next suite where Scott—the new guy, is holding the door open for us as we go in to see two young girls and their families waiting. My band is already here and have been telling the girls cool stories about being on the road with me.

"And would ya look at that, your favorite person in the world just walked through the door," my guitar player says. Everyone's heads turn to see me, less pageantry than they're used to seeing me in, but their shrieks might indicate that they don't care. "And just like that, I'm no longer the most interesting person in the room," he says with a grin. "It's really nice meeting you two lovely ladies. Enjoy the rest of your night." He shakes the parents' hands and the girls give him a hug.

"Hey guys! It's so cool to finally meet you!" I tell them with as much enthusiasm as I can muster. I'm tired, but also this is genuine. I get so much out of taking time to meet my fans. I fill my cup when I learn their stories and it inspires me and always recharges me in a way that not many things can.

"Oh my God!" they both squeal in a tandem of screams.

The two girls jump up and down with an outburst of excitement. I'm shocked that they can have any energy left if they were anything like this while watching my three hour performance.

"It's you! It's really you!" one girl says.

"Yes, it's me, it's me. I'm really me." I can't help but to laugh. I'm guessing she is nine or ten years old. "What's your name?"

"Ohmygod, ohmygod!"

"Take a breath, honey," a woman says to her, gently.

The girl hugs me, her arms locked around my waist. "My name is Sara."

The other girl steps forward as well and I reach out to pull her in as well. "It's nice to meet you Sara," I say, with my hand on her back. I look at the other girl. "What's your name?"

The other girl is shy, but I can see the excitement in her eyes. She's fighting a smile. Happy tears go with a thin lip-stretched grin as she tries to contain her excitement. "Jude."

"Jude, that's a pretty name." I pull her into the group hug for a moment. "I love your scarf. It matches one of my outfits I wore on stage." I notice the scarf covering her head.

"Thank you," Jude says, barely audible.

"I can't believe it's really you!" Sara says with emotions gripping her voice. She pulls away and looks back at her mom. "Mommy! It's actually Phoebe Fox!"

"Yeah, it sure is. Tell her how much you loved the show."

Sara turns back to me, "Ohmygosh! You were so good! I loved the show! It was so amazing!"

"Yeah? What was your favorite part of the show?"

"I loved when you sang *Girl's World*, and had the big suit on and the stage raised up like a building. And the dancers were so cool, too!"

She talks fast and it's hard to not laugh. I live for this.

"I'm so happy you loved that song. That is one of my favorite songs to play," I tell Sara. "It's so cool that I get to sing it with the best dancers in the world too!"

Sara's eyes are big and bright and she's adorable with her freckles. "Yeah! I wanna be a dancer for you one day!"

I try to maintain the smile, but knowing that these very special meets are because these kids are usually terminal makes it tough sometimes. I love doing these, but when kids say stuff like that, it breaks my heart into a million little pieces and leaves me pretending that I'm a more optimistic version of myself. "That's awesome! You know, I'm always looking for great dancers, too!"

"She is always dancing to your songs in her room," her mother says. "When she has the energy at least."

I look over to Jude with the most disarming smile I can offer. "What about you? What was your favorite part of the show?"

Sara looks back at her parents, smiling and jumping. Jude ponders with her lips twisted, deep in thought.

"Did you see my shirt?" Sara asks, still overflowing with joy while Jude continues to stare at the floor. It's a soft blue t-shirt with me on the front that Sara is wearing, looking more sexual than I'm proud of—considering a child is wearing it—but her excitement makes me giddy.

"I did! I love it! *I* don't even have that shirt!"

"I liked *Out of the Dark*!" Jude spouts, reclaiming the conversation. "It's my favorite song." Something about how she said it, how she took her time to tell me, and how her eyes hold mine tells me that it's more special to her than just a catchy chorus.

"Oh yeah? That one isn't even on the radio. Tell me what it is about *that* song that you love."

"Oooo! I like that one too!" Sara says. Everyone is all smiles as the three of us talk.

The parents talk amongst themselves. My security hangs back, as they normally do every night after the show for these more intimate meets. I crouch down and take each of their hands, looking them both in the eye on their level. "So that song is very special to me. Do you know what it's about?" I ask the two.

They both look at each other and don't really say they do, and I can tell they don't.

"I'm gonna let you both in on the secret," I say, lowering my voice. "I think most people make their own interpretation of the song and assume it's about a breakup with a boy, but it's actually about me fighting through all of the bad things people say about me. On TV, the internet, or in magazines. It's just about me not letting any haters stop me from being myself and being happy. It's my song to the bullies."

Sara looks like I just blew her mind. Her cheeks are tight and I can see her dimples. Her eyes wide and in awe after hearing my *secret*. "Okay, that's really cool."

"Can I tell you why I love that song?" Jude asks.

"Of course!" I say. I stare at her eagerly, waiting for her soft-spoken words to tumble out of her mouth with something profound.

"It sounds like you're sad at first, but then the music goes from pretty to heavy and you sound angry, and you talk about getting through anything in your way no matter what." So far she's right on point. "And by the end, it makes me feel good."

"Well, that's awesome, I'm glad to hear it makes you feel good!"

"Yeah, it just makes me feel like," her voice begins to tremble a bit. A sniffle escapes her nose as she looks down at the floor.

I squeeze her hand a little tighter, and even though Sara is looking at her too, for a moment I try to make it feel like it's just me and Jude.

"Hey, talk to me. It's okay. It's just you and me, Jude." I can see the tears in her eyes filling up and threatening to spill.

She pulls in a deep breath. "It just makes me feel like, if you can get through anything, then maybe I can too."

There it is.

Absolutely shattered.

Sara throws an arm around her and hugs her, but Jude and I stay locked eye to eye and I'm sure she can see my eyes start to water now.

Dammit.

I wasn't trying to cry here. This sweet little girl is fighting for her life and meeting me was her one wish.

I need to be strong for her.

"Listen to me," I can feel my voice shaking now, betraying this little girl's hero. I don't even begin to know how to be someone's hero, but I try to play the part the best I can. "I know I don't know what you're going through, but I want you to know that you're not alone in your fight. Okay?"

Jude nods. I look at Sara as well as to not ignore her fight. I'm not sure what Sara's story is, but I want to keep it light so I typically try to just be in the moment and be the person everyone expects when they meet me. I was a little girl once and remember how powerful it can be to meet someone famous. "You're not alone either, Sara."

We three hold hands in a makeshift circle while I'm still crouched down—and a little uncomfortable—but I don't want to ruin this moment for them. Hell, for me either. Jude just broke me completely and I just want to go lay in bed and have a good cry now.

"You know . . . you win some, and you lose some. But if you keep fighting and you go down swinging, you can feel good knowing that even though you're scared, that you're not going down quietly. You're so brave and it's girls like you two that are heroes to *me*."

Sara and Jude both listen, hanging onto my every word. It's just us in our little circle right now. Our private little moment that means everything to us all in our little corner of the world.

"Can I make you both a promise?"

They look at each other and then turn to me. Sara shakes her head and Jude's eyebrows raise eagerly for what I say next.

"The next time I sing that song, no matter where I'm at, I'm gonna be thinking of you two." They both smile. Jude with a shy grin impossible to tame, and Sara with joyful eyes that make me smile. "The next time I perform it on stage . . . it's for you two."

I'm careful to include them both, but I make sure to look Jude in the eyes when I say it.

"So when I sing it, I'll be saying your names," I look over to the girls' parents while I'm still talking to them. "And your parents can watch for the clips on social media and maybe share with you very soon, how does that sound?"

The girls smile harder somehow, I've not seen their faces not smiling since I walked in. "Yes!" Sara shouts. Jude grins, holding eye contact with me.

Their parents smile and nod their heads, understanding. One of the mothers mouths the words *thank you* and her kind eyes make it feel that much heavier.

"I see you both have all those friendship bracelets!" I say, my voice going up an octave to be more cheery. "You both have all of the prettiest bracelets!"

"Thank you!" Sara says.

Jude holds her arm out and twists it to show off the many colors. The plastic beads clack softly with her movement.

"Did you guys make these yourselves?"

"Some of them I traded tonight, but some of them I made," Jude says.

"Yeah, me too," Sara adds.

"Well, let's do this. We're all friends now, right? Can I call you both my friends?" I ask as I pull two bracelets off my wrist. The girls nod yes as I hold out soft pink and black beaded bracelets with glittery stars on them to each. "I want to swap a bracelet with each of you if that's okay, but only the ones you made. Deal?"

Both of their eyes light up and Sara is quick to roll a bunch of them off of her arm and lays them out on the floor to decide which one she wants me to have. Jude is staring at her arm a little more calculated in her decision.

Sara is quick to hand me a bracelet that is orange and green and white beads, which seems fitting considering we're in Ireland. "Thank you so much, it's beautiful," I say as I hand her my bracelet and slide hers onto my other wrist.

"You're welcome. Thank you!" Sara says.

I look back at Jude as she looks to be still deciding. "Which one are you thinking?"

"I don't know. I'm still deciding," Jude says, clearly overthinking this exchange. I admire her thoughtfulness.

She grabs one with blue and white beads. The white beads have letters on them that spell something out. She hands me the bracelet and takes the one I offer. "Thank you. It's very pretty," I say as I look at it closer and see what it says.

*S*T*R*O*N*G**E*N*O*U*G*H*

Well, there it is. I'm definitely going to cry again.

Yep, I can feel it. I get goosebumps as I read the letters and I clutch it in my fist and close my eyes for a moment to try and control myself. She needs those words more than I do, but the weight of her story and everything is so heavy. For her to feel like it's appropriate for me to have this beats my soul into submission.

I slip the bracelet onto my wrist and pull her in for a long hug as I stand up. Her head rests against my chest and I try not to cry. I pull Sara in as well and we have our moment. "Thank you so much . . . both of you. These bracelets mean the world to me and I am so happy I could meet you tonight . . . thank you."

@queenie_b_xoxo: HOLY SHIT! BEST NIGHT EVER!

@phoebefan2002: BEST CONCERT I'VE EVER SEEN!

@iheartgudmuzik: So much better in person than a screen! I don't even have words.

@cam_michellezzz: Show me another singer putting on that kind of show! So much better than I could have ever dreamed! **#PhoebeFoxLive #PhoebeFox #ThroughTheYearsTour #LiveMusic**

@truckingrightalong: My wife dragged me out to this expensive concert tonight but I'm kind of glad I came. Pretty good show! She's happy.

@Dancinginthenight_: **@PhoebeFox** Thank you so much for playing all of my favorite songs! You're amazing!

@sun.child99: Screaming. Crying. Throwing up. **#PhoebeFoxTour**

@irishgirlie1213: Ireland really showed up tonight for Phoebe! Erin go braugh!

@parallel_lines1: My bestie and I flew all the way from the US – no regrets! Experience of a lifetime. No one does it like Phoebe Fox. Period. **#foxieforlife**

After I have my moment with Jude and Sara, we hug each other so tight and the feeling never gets old. I take photos with everyone and chat with the families briefly. Everyone is so grateful to meet me and I understand the platform I'm on, I really do, but it still feels weird sometimes. This is one of those times.

My assistant tells me that they're fueling up the private jet now and that we should be on our way to the airstrip soon. I say my farewells and my security team leads me out as we move our feet down the corridor once more.

Jack and Aaron stay in front while Harry and Scott follow behind my assistant and I.

"That was really beautiful in there, Miss Fox."

"Phoebe," I reply, correcting her. "And yeah, they were so sweet."

"Okay, so when you touch down in the Netherlands, you'll have a luxury SUV pick up waiting on the airstrip to avoid more inter-action than you would like. I asked for a van to accommodate your carry-on luggage and your protection detail. It will go directly to a private estate reserved for you."

"Got it, thank you," I say. We walk for roughly ten minutes before being led into the team parking garage where a large sprinter van is waiting to take my four bodyguards and me to the airport. I climb into the back, claiming dibs on a window seat—not that it matters, the windows are tinted, and it's night time—and my team piles into the van accordingly. Same ole, same ole.

The door shuts and the five of us are whisked away through the streets of Ireland as I stare out the window at indistinguishable buildings and lights. It's not long before I pull out my phone and go to Instagram and see the overwhelming amount of tags in fan posts. I wish I could look at all of these but the volume is staggering and impossible to keep up with. I close Instagram within seconds.

I stare at my Home screen and see my cat, Paw McGraw, and I miss him so much. I haven't been home much lately. This tour has been a lot, and with me in the studio so much between legs of this tour, I am struggling. I haven't spoken to my mom as much as I normally like and I feel like I need to make it a point to see her soon. Maybe after this next show I will see what I can have arranged. My best friends, Hanna and Naomi, I've managed to keep in touch with, mostly through the three of us sharing memes and funny videos in a group chat. I would love to make time to go visit them and just hang out without the obligation to be somewhere.

Since I started re-recording my music a few years back, the amount of time spent at the studio has made it like a second home. Compound that with writing new music as well . . . ya girl is flippin' *tired*.

The car ride is quiet for a majority of the time, until Harry speaks up. "Have any of you been to the Red Light district?"

Jack snickers beside me as he leans forward to listen to Harry. "It's been a while, but yeah. You lookin' to wet yer' whistle, brother?"

Aaron laughs. "I haven't, but we really won't have a lot of time there for that sort of thing, ya know, since we're on the clock."

Aaron and Jack have been with me for a majority of my touring life. Around the time I got my first Grammy, if I remember right.

Aaron likes to assert himself as the boss without calling himself that, but I'd say he is the apparent alpha.

"Why would you ask that right now, anyway, you dumbass?" Jack smacks Harry playfully in the back of his head, hard enough to make a meaty *smack* sound. "Phoebe is sitting right here," he gestures to me. "Why would you think she would wanna hear that shit?"

I stare at Harry, amused. This is reminiscent of riding the school bus when I was in grade school, only now the boys are men with muscles and a little thunder in their chests. I can't help but to laugh. These guys, all like protective brothers to me. Protective and at times, a bit of middle-school boy energy. Rough-housing and crude jokes are never off the table, so long as it's in a private setting like this. Aaron and Jack are married, happily. Harry, I believe, is seeing someone, but I'm not sure if it's serious. I just know that I've never felt uncomfortable around them, ever. Scott is single, and what's important is that all of them are professionals when it matters most. I just let the boys be boys and smile through it more often than not.

"Okay, okay, jeez," Harry grins. He smacks Scott on the chest. "Come on man, back me up, New Guy."

"Ay, ay, ay, don't go bringin' New Guy into this," Aaron says.

"Guys, I've been here for over six months now," Scott interrupts. "We've literally traveled the whole United States and Canada, I think I've earned a better name than–"

"Look at that, you ass," Jack interjects with his deep bass heavy voice. "You went and irritated the new guy."

Aaron, Jack, and Harry all laugh while Scott stares quietly. Clearly annoyed at the hazing.

'Well," Harry starts. "Do you think a lady can be sent to my room?"

"Dude!"

"Shut up!"

"Don't you have a woman back home?"

All of the guys shout at once and Harry shuts down, laughing at himself. "Okay, okay . . . no lucky ladies then. Got it. Loud and clear." The silence in the van is broken only by the passing traffic and wind hitting the vehicle as we roll along. "Aaron, what are you doing later to–"

Aaron smacks Harry upside the head and the two laugh.

This is typical behavior with these boys. Thankfully they do their job well when it's showtime and I love them all. I'd be lying if I said I wasn't at least entertained.

The van approaches the airport and we're led onto the airstrip by a convoy of cars. It isn't long before we all climb out of the van with the tarmac under our feet and the scenic view of planes moving on and off the runway.

"Miss Fox," a man in a fancy navy blue v-neck sweater walks up to me, his hand on his hat so the wind doesn't carry it away with the next flight taking off. He raises his voice to talk over the wind and the hum of the engines. "Your jet is almost ready! I'm Captain Lopez! I'll be your pilot this evening! Heading to the Netherlands!? Have you ever been!?"

"I have!" I shout.

"Perfect! I assumed you probably had. Hard not to know who you are, Miss Fox! My daughters are huge fans!"

"Thank you!" I shout once more.

"We're gonna get you boarded shortly and get you there safely!" He nods with a smile and heads back to the plane.

"What's the plan?" Jack hollers.

The rest of the team gathers around. "That was the pilot!" I shout. "He said it will just be a minute."

As I'm talking, a woman in all white approaches us. "Miss Fox, you and your party are clear to board."

"Thank you!" I shout. The fellas all nod and fall into formation. Two in front of me, and two behind me.

The woman follows alongside me. "My name is Maeve and I'll be your flight attendant for this trip!"

"Nice to meet you Maeve!" I say over the noise.

"Right this way, Miss Fox. I'm a massive fan. I started listening to you as a young girl. It's an honor to meet you."

That is still a weird concept to me. I've been doing this so long that there are women out here who grew up listening to me. Like, *real* adults in the *real* world functioning. I can't help but feel her endearing comment like a dagger in my chest, telling me I'm getting old as it plunges deeper. But I don't tell her this . . . instead I just smile politely.

We step onto the airstairs and one by one we each file into the cabin where we're greeted individually by the captain, the co-pilot, Maeve, and another flight attendant.

We're all quick to take our seats. The boys are always happy to fly private. I have to admit, the extra legroom and clean leather seats are a bit *bougie*, but if I'm as high profile as I'm made to feel, then why shouldn't I make the expense to be comfortable? When you fly as much as we do—especially on tour—you suddenly reframe your willingness to spend money on things like private jets and luxury stays at private villas.

"Time to kick off the shoes and watch a movie," Harry says as he plops into one of the recliners near the back. He slides off his shoes with ease.

"Bro, your feet better not stink this time," Jack says, all of the gruff in his voice.

"Yeah, that shit was foul back in London," Aaron says with an edge to his voice. "If I even get a whiff of sweaty socks, I swear to Christ, I'll toss you out of the plane myself."

Harry laughs as he leans back and his footrest flings out. "Fuck off, mate!" he says in a terrible—likely offensive—British accent as he whips a throw pillow at Aaron that makes him flinch.

"Now, now boys, isn't it about your guys' bedtimes?" I ask with a sarcastic and motherly tone.

Aaron picks up the pillow and smacks Scott with it. "Yeah, isn't it your bedtime, New Guy?"

Scott snatches the pillow and tosses it into an empty recliner. "I haven't had a bed time since I was a child."

Jack plops into the seat where Scott threw the pillow. "You mean you're not a child?" he asks with a smirk.

I take my seat as the banter continues among the guys.

The flight attendant who isn't Maeve comes up to me as I am pulling my phone out. "Hi Miss Fox, my name is Ruth. Can I get you anything before we take off?"

I smile at her as I put my AirPods in my ears. "Yes, may I have water please?"

"Right away," she says as she heads to the back of the plane.

I put on the music and despite the short flight that is only expected to be ninety minutes or so, I try to get some form of a nap in. After performing for three hours and all of the festivities afterward, sitting down and getting comfortable really lets the fatigue settle into my bones. My friend, Naomi Wilde, just released a new song last week and I've been obsessed with it. She has been crushing it and I'm looking forward to having her open for me when I'm back in the states.

Ruth brings my water in a glass bottle and places it in the cupholder at my side. "Thank you," I say, unable to hear her as bass notes beat in my ears. I slide an eye mask over my eyes and try to relax. The music pulls me into a warm and cozy headspace and before I fall away into dreamland I feel the plane engines roaring through the vibration of the seat. The movement is obvious but I've grown so accustomed to takeoffs that I can tell when we're in the air and when we're taking off without looking out the windows.

I take a drink of the water and set it back in the cupholder and the soft music plays in my ears, where a gritty but beautiful voice of someone I adore sings me a song that I can fall asleep to.

5

I crawl out of a deep sleep to a hand on my shoulder, jostling me. I pull my AirPods from my ears to not be so immersed in the sudden transition to Electronica music that definitely wasn't the vibe I fell asleep to. I raise the mask from my eyes and see Harry there, "Pheebs, almost there, you should probably wake up."

I clear my throat. "Yeah, okay . . . thanks."

I take a drink of water as the pilot's voice comes onto the speaker.

"We're just about ten minutes out and we are clear to begin our descent. Should have no problems landing in Amsterdam. Please remain seated and we will get you back on the ground, safely."

As I'm prying my tired eyes open for the landing, it's four in the morning and all I'm thinking about is getting to the villa and passing out. No shower. Nothing! Just bed, and sleep.

The boys are going back and forth about past times they had to restrain people at shows. These discussions are always amusing because they all talk about it the same way military veterans reminisce about war time.

"Yeah," Jack is saying. "I still think it's a crock that we aren't allowed to use handcuffs anymore."

"I don't remember a time where I ever carried handcuffs," Aaron interjects.

"All because one whiny old woman," Jack continues, "doesn't know how to follow the rules to begin with and chose to complain about it, even though I gave more than plenty of warning and chances to chill the fuck out."

I know my place when they get like this. It starts with these guys swapping stories, then it turns into a pissing contest somehow. I can't help but to laugh sometimes.

"Sometimes people want you to give them something to complain about," Scott says.

"Yeah, New Guy is right," Aaron adds. "Some people just want a cool story to tell when a celebrity's name comes up. Just how some people are, even if it's not them in the best light."

He's not wrong. I've been on the receiving end of this more times than I can count.

Scott rolls his eyes. "I honestly prefer zip ties anyway."

"How can you even say that when you never got to use the cuffs, though?" Jack asks, ready to die on that hill from the sound of his voice.

"You can carry a lot more zip ties at once, and they're easier to break if you misplace the key," Scott argues.

"Why would I misplace the key? If I'm a professional," Jack uses air quotes when he says *professional*, "I'm not losing the key, brother."

"You can lose that key and you're up shit's creek," Scott continues. "Plus, I always go back to the old adage. Failing to prepare is preparing to fail. Why would I want to be worrying about a key?"

I've gotta say, Scott sounds wise beyond his years when he puts it like that.

"I think I'm with Scotty on this one," Harry interjects.

"I thought I was New Guy?" Scott says.

"You are!" Aaron confirms.

I try to fight back laughing out loud. Sometimes I can't help but to crack a smile. I don't support hazing, but I can appreciate good fun. Besides, Scott seems like he has thick enough skin.

"Stop, you're gonna confuse Scotty," Harry jabs.

"So I'm Scotty?" Scott asks.

"No!" Jack and Aaron say in chorus.

I laugh out loud and a big yawn comes over me.

"The metal cuffs are heavier and make a lot of noise if you carry more than one pair. You can carry a fifty pack of zip ties and use a pocket knife instead of a key," Harry says, supporting Scott's thoughts on zip ties versus handcuffs.

"Yeah," Jack begins." That's true but if you slap a set of steel cuffs on some scumbag's wrist, they aren't getting out of those bad boys."

"You aren't getting out of the zip ties either," Scott argues.

"We are on the descent. Please remain seated and keep your seatbelts fastened," the pilot says over the speaker.

"Actually," Aaron offers, grunting with a grin on his face. "You can get out of zip ties fairly easily."

Jack twists his lips and gestures a hand to Aaron while nodding.

"How do you figure?" Harry asks. Scott looks on, suspicious of whatever Aaron might say next.

"It's super simple really," Aaron starts. "New Guy . . . pass me a couple zip ties, would ya?"

Scott pulls a couple of clear zip ties from his carry-on at his feet and leans forward to pass them off to Aaron.

And here it is. The pissing contest portion of the boys arguing over nothing.

"I'll show you once we land, I need to stand for this," Aaron says.

I rub my eyes and yawn with a stretch as the plane lands. Only a couple of minutes before we're given the green light to step out. As our feet touch the tarmac in the Netherlands, a black SUV is parked and waiting. Morning approaches and the world outside is still dark, but the cool air somehow just feels like morning.

"Okay, hold on now," Scott says, with Harry beside him. Aaron and Jack look at him. "Show us now."

"Alright," Aaron says. He hands a zip tie to Jack. "Take me to jail, boss."

Jack reluctantly takes the zip tie and fastens Aaron's wrists together. "Good?"

Aaron smiles. "Perfect!"

"And you didn't start compromising the plastic?" Harry asked, his words laced with suspicion.

Aaron offers up his wrists. "See for yourself. Go ahead, give it a tug."

Scott inspects the zip tie and gives a nod of approval. "Looks good . . . do your magic, Houdini."

"Sick burn, New Guy!" Harry says, hand raised for a high five.

"I thought you were calling me Scotty," Scott says, staring at Harry's raised hand.

"Come on," Harry says. "Don't leave me hanging."

"So, what you want to do to get out of this is," Aaron starts, demonstrating with his tethered fists raised above his head. "Raise your hands as high up as you can, like this." He tightens his fists and rotates them close together. "You want to try and separate your wrists as much as you can. Really put as much pressure on the tie as you can. Now, it's going to chew into your skin a little bit but if you're quick," Aaron moves his hands down so fast. I forget he can move that fast sometimes. The zip tie breaks, just as easy as he said it would. "You can bring it down against your hip and the tension you add to it from your forearms or wrist are enough to make these things snap like dry spaghetti."

Jack looks impressed. "That's why I prefer handcuffs."

"Wow, I kind of thought you were full of shit," Harry says, lowering his hand as he gives up on the high five that Scott refuses to give.

"Yeah, I told ya," Aaron says, picking up the broken zip tie. "It's so easy a girl could do it." Aaron hands me the other zip tie. "Go ahead, Pheebs, try it."

I'm way too tired for this, and so uninterested in this petty boy argument. "No, I don't want to," I say.

"See, not *so easy a girl could do it* after all, is it?" Harry asks.

If there is one thing I hate, it's being told I can't do something. And just because I'm a woman only adds to the fire. Now being tired and fantasizing about how soft the bed is has to take a backseat to this stupid squabble. "You know what," I say. "I'll do it." I hold my hands out in front of me with my wrists pressed together.

Aaron fastens it to my wrists. "That too tight?" he asks.

"Do you ask people if it's too tight, normally?" I ask with a tinge of attitude.

"You're right, you're right," Aaron says. "Okay . . . you remember what I said?"

I stare at him as he coaches me through the great escape that is a cheap plastic zip tie. "I think so."

"Hands high above your head." He raises his hands along with me. I follow along, like a weird game of *Simon says*. "Then, you're gonna start to separate your wrists and really put as much tension on the tie as you can." His forearms flex as he strains, even in his unrestrained demonstration.

I am doing as he says and the zip tie really does hurt. They dig into my skin and feel like rug burn as the plastic is tight against my tender skin. It feels like it will leave a bruise and I'm feeling even more like this is stupid.

"Then as you're trying to stretch the zip tie, bring it down as fast and as hard as you can while trying to break free. Bring it down on your hip, or wherever the hardest part of your body is that you can use." He does the motion twice while explaining. He moves so fast and I flinch the first time he does it.

I take a deep breath through my nose and my face hardens like steel. I swing my fists down toward my hip as I scream. The zip tie snaps way easier than I expected. The boys clap and cheer as I look at my wrists and see the bright redness from the pressure. I can't help the dorky grin on my face, surprised at how simple that was. I do feel like my hip is going to be bruised in the morning, well . . . the afternoon, maybe.

"See," Aaron says as he throws an arm around me. I rub my wrist, giving him a side eye glance. "So easy, even a girl can do it."

The Rise of Phoebe Fox - Part 1

[The documentary opens with dramatic music playing. Booming sounds set the tone against the visual of a fit woman wearing tight shorts and a sports bra in frame under a black and white filter. The camera is careful never to show her face. She begins sprinting in slow motion.]

There are a lot of us who see a celebrity or a performer living their dream for our entertainment. As the consumers, we often only see what we're shown, but not the seeds being planted before the sprouting of the fruitful tree we grow to love. We pick those fruits and harvest everything the tree gives us until its branches are bare. Some of us choose to turn on the tree once it has nothing left to give, others would rather cut it down and dig up the roots only to leave it in obscurity. And then some of us are more willing to water the tree, showing patience while appreciating the fruits the bare tree once gave us.

[The woman runs up a hill. Close-up shots show her muscular toned legs fighting to climb. She reaches the top and collapses under a tree, resting her back against it. Close up of the sweat on her collarbone.]

Can you appreciate progress without struggle?

Can you harness growth without resistance?

Can you appreciate love without hate?

[A modest film reel shows a neighborhood. B-roll
footage of cars passing and stop lights are shown
before stopping on a residential home. That home
would be where Phoebe grew up for a majority of her
childhood.]

*From a young age, Phoebe Fox knew her talent was
too big for just playing songs in her bedroom on a
second-hand guitar. She knew if she was ever going
to be taken seriously that she would have to go
out into the world and find a stage of her own. But
with that stage will come an audience with a lot of
different eyes and a lot of different voices. More
voices sometimes means more opportunities, but also
. . . obstacles to conquer.*

*From a small-town girl with ambitions and drive
greater than the average . . . to becoming a cultural
icon in music.*

This is her story.

This is her journey through adversity.

This is . . . the rise of Phoebe Fox.

[In what looks like a living room, an older woman
in a light gray sweater and thin gold necklace
with a small cross pendant sits down, adjusting
herself as voices off camera instruct her. She
has a seat on a white couch with a colorful throw
blanket draped over the back, and smiles at the
camera.]

                    Martha Fox
My name is Martha Fox, and I am Phoebe's mom.
She's been my best friend from the moment she
                came into this world.

                    Interviewer
Can you talk about Phoebe's first time performing
                for an audience?

                    Martha Fox
Yes. Wait, do you mean in front of a school?

                    Interviewer
Maybe more of her on her own in pursuit of her
                    dream.

                    Martha Fox
Oh, yes. Well, Phoebe was probably thirteen, almost
fourteen. We had all just moved to Tennessee, her

daddy took a job there and as fate would have it,
we were not too far from Nashville.

*Nashville is understood to be the launchpad for so
many musicians in the industry today. In a town
bustling with creativity it's only matched by the
hunger from those who are willing to starve just to
express themselves in front of an audience. Its rich
history and promise of opportunity is too appealing
to overlook. For many performers being drawn to the
spotlight, like Phoebe, all they would need is a
chance.*

Martha Fox

I became Phoebe's manager by default at that time.
Driving around my teen daughter, I had to be sure
she was safe first and foremost. I'd heard stories
about greedy people taking advantage of grown-ups
so I was always a bit protective of her when she
had opportunities.

Her first official gig as Phoebe Fox was at the
Grand Ole Opry Mall.

[Soft music plays over a home video footage montage
of a young Phoebe smiling for the shaky camera as she
carries a guitar. Her mother walks beside her as the
camera follows along a driveway just as Phoebe opens
the back door to a car and lays the guitar across
the backseat and laughs at the camera. Everyone gets
into the car and Phoebe sits in the front passenger
seat, turning back with a serious face as she looks

into the camera, fighting the creeping smirk just
before breaking into laughter.]

Martha Fox
It was right in the center of the mall, right smack
dab in the middle of everything. Anyone there could
just be walking by and see performers all day.
Chairs were open to anyone and that just didn't
exist where we came from. I remember sitting beside
her, she was so nervous sitting there in her flowery
sundress and big boots with her acoustic guitar and
the bedazzled strap.

[Home video plays from the seats in the mall,
showing a young boy on stage singing. The camera
swings over to Martha and Phoebe. Phoebe gazes
toward the stage with her guitar standing on the
floor and the neck in her hand.]

Martha Fox
We watched a young boy playing just before she went
up. He was doing a little bit of country and a little
bit of indie, but he sounded amazing. He seemed
like he was right out of high school maybe. He gave
this speech near the end that I know resonated with
Phoebe. I know because we talked about it on the
drive home after. He talked about how scary it was
to be playing in front of all of the people, but how
his dream to sing and travel outweighed any fears
he had about singing in front of anyone. He said he
had a dream that he's been wanting to chase since
he was a boy and how he was honored to be able to
chase that dream that day.

[The home video shows the boy walking off the stage and waving to the crowd with a single hand and a nod with the biggest glowing grin on his face.]

                        Martha Fox
    He got an applause from the dozens of people standing and sitting who were watching him. He went into his closing song, a catchy cover of a country song.

Following a passionate musician in a similar position as Phoebe was not much help for her nerves, but she was determined not to fail.

                        Martha Fox
    So the boy exits the stage and a guy comes up and gives Phoebe a . . . less than passionate introduction.

[A shot of an empty chair in a dramatically lit studio space sits to the right of the frame as a woman with long blonde hair steps onto the set and has a seat. It's Phoebe Fox in a bright floral sundress, smiling.]

                        Interviewer
So your mother was telling us a bit about your first time performing at the Grand Ole Opry. Do you think you could tell us a bit about what that was like for you?

                           Phoebe Fox
                   Oh, God . . . I was a wreck.
                       (audible laughter)
It was quite the experience for a fourteen year
old girl. I had watched so many live performances
on the internet in my room. I had practiced in
front of a mirror so many times alone, but . . .
it's never exactly what you think it's going to
be when you are used to playing in your room. I
went up on the stage and I stood there in front
of the mic stand, my guitar hanging. There were
maybe twenty, thirty people sitting around the
                      stage, spread out.

                           Interviewer
           You've come a long way since then, huh?

                           Phoebe Fox
                       (audible laughter)
. . . I'd say a very long way, yeah. Anyway, I
could kind of tell who the audience was before
I got on stage. People were stopping while their
spouses shopped. People sat to rest, not really
paying attention to the musicians. I'd say about
half of the people there were actually engaged
and watching. Oh! It was funny too, I can actually
remember when I introduced myself, how my voice
cracked a little when I was trying to adjust the
microphone. I actually watched a man roll his
                  eyes, get up and leave.

Interviewer
Wow! Do you think he has any clue who you would
become?

Phoebe Fox
Well . . . joke's on him, I guess. I remember
feeling very discouraged at that moment. Before I
even played a single chord, I had the thought to
just quit right there.

Interviewer
What kept you from it?

Phoebe Fox
My mom. I stood there with eyes on me, waiting for
me to do my party trick and as I looked around,
I saw my mom there. She smiled at me and I could
read it on her face. She reassured me with just a
look and I knew in my heart, at that moment, that
this was what I came to do. The set started off a
bit rough. It wasn't like I got to practice on that
stage with those acoustics before. We just showed
up and my mom signed me up.

Martha Fox
Oh, she was great. It was incredible watching her
for the first time like that. She seemed nervous
for a second but it seemed like once she started
playing music, all of that melted. She was a star.
Her voice was incredible. She was nailing it. But I
guess she could feel the crowd not really into it.
She switched from country to rock. Now, you have to

understand, I've listened to her at home playing for years and it's mostly ever been country. I was just as surprised as everyone else there when she played Simple Man by Lynard Skynard. She did a beautiful acoustic rendition of it and that's when the crowd seemed to come around.

Interviewer
I would love to have seen that. It's difficult to even imagine her doing that today.

Martha Fox
So she finishes her last song and as she is coming off stage, I watch a mother with a baby stop her in the aisle way.

Interviewer
Your mom told us about after that performance how people stopped you as you came off the stage. What sort of things did you hear?

Phoebe Fox
One woman told me how beautiful I sounded and how she was glad she stayed to listen. It was nice to hear that right away. I needed that. Before I could see my mom, the boy who was up before me stopped me.

Interviewer
What did he say to you?

Phoebe Fox

He just gave me words of encouragement. He was very
kind and complimentary when he didn't have to be.
I really appreciated hearing that. He gave me some
tips on stage presence and afterward it was all I
could think about before I went home and sang in
front of the mirror again.

Martha Fox

He told her to keep at it and when we finished
she was just beaming. Her smile could have lit the
stage.

Phoebe Fox

I went up to my mom and hugged her so tight. She
hugged me even tighter. That's my best friend, you
know? She has always been my biggest supporter.

[A video plays of Phoebe and her mom side by side
in a more recent video backstage after a concert.
The two smile and hug as Martha tells Phoebe how
great she was out there.]

6

The five of us all climb into the vehicle. Typically I always go for the rearmost seat in an SUV. The fellas pile in and the driver is quick about getting us moving.

"Just so you all know, uh," the driver speaks with a thick accent while he stumbles through his English. "The, uh, how do you say, the home is, uhhhh, it's twenty-five minutes."

"Thank you," I say from the backseat. I lock eyes with him as he looks into the rearview mirror. The tinted windows, even from the inside, make the outside morning seem so much darker than it actually is. I expect it to be daylight before I get into this place.

"You're uhhh," the driver starts. He snaps his fingers several times in succession as he stammers through his thoughts, struggling to find the English words for what he wants to say. "You're on tour, yes?"

"Mhm," I say, nodding and still meeting his eyes in the rearview mirror. "Yes."

"Big, big star. Superstar," he says with high eyebrows and a wide smile.

I smile and nod politely.

I see excitement on his face. It's a familiar excitement. The driver is starstruck. "Mijn vrouw houdt van je muziek. Grote fan."

I stare at him, frozen as he reaches for the words in English but only offers them in Dutch . . . I think. Jack looks back at me with a coy smile as I sit here with a stupefied look on my face. "I'm sorry, I don't speak–"

"Zij zal aanwezig zijn op uw show in Amsterdam," he interrupts me, with more words that make me feel even more lost. Traveling internationally isn't as bad as it sounds really—considering I have a team of assistants and security around me at all times—but every so often, like now, I find myself challenged with my own ignorance of the native tongues and my surroundings. It makes me feel small to wonder how I would manage if I were alone here.

Jack leans forward, practically over the driver's shoulder. "Phoebe spreekt geen Nederlands. Ik zal het haar vertellen."

The driver stares at me in the mirror as he listens to whatever Jack just said. His smile still wore just as big on his friendly face.

"What was that?" I ask, whispering to Jack as I lean forward.

He leans back, lowering his voice. "The driver just says that his wife is a big fan. She will be at your show in Amsterdam, and I told him you don't speak the language."

"Oh," I say, leaning back. The driver's hands on the wheel, SUV in motion, and his eyes still darting to me from the road to the mirror. "Thank you."

I smile big. This is a little uncomfortable, but usually harmless. Not uncommon at all. Harry and Aaron seem to have fallen asleep almost as fast as the car began moving. Scott sits up, hyper-aware, his head on a swivel. He must have had caffeine or slept well enough on the plane because he seems a little wired, like he's looking for trouble. I guess *one* of my bodyguards should be so alert. I get it. I only have caffeine in coffee usually and too much can make me anxious too.

I stare out the window feeling the exhaustion in my bones. I could sink into the upholstery and fall asleep right now. I gaze through the thick window tint at the industrial landscape for a few minutes. Daybreak lightens up the surroundings and it's not long before we're on a quiet road with farm style fences and trees on both sides.

The world passes by at a comfortable speed and my childhood bestie, Hanna, pops into my mind. I'm longing for an evening where we can hang out and just goof off, like when we were teenagers. One of the first things I plan to do when this tour is over is to fly her to my house, eat greasy takeout and candy while we watch cheesy rom coms and just enjoy one another. Having a stretch on my calendar where I have nowhere to be is really all I'm wanting right now. Not that I'm ungrateful at all for the present moment, but sometimes when I'm feeling run down it just feels like I'm enduring.

While I'm staring out the window and caught in my head I'm noticing how Harry and Aaron fell asleep so fast, I'm not much better. In my deep thought my tired body is sung to sleep by the white noise of the soft motor humming and the road passing underneath us. The scenery whizzing by under the morning sun doesn't help either. Feeling that warm sun like a soft kiss, even behind my closed eyes. My passive thoughts bleed into that strange space between awake and dreaming.

I'm comfortable.

My body is at rest.

I'm completely relaxed.

My mind is slowing down.

I can breathe.

That warm sun peeking over the horizon reminds me of sitting on the porch at my parents house as a kid. Strumming an acoustic guitar while my bare feet are pressed against the warm sun-kissed wood of the steps that the awning didn't cover.

Warm.

Comfortable.

Slipping further into the soft sound of the strings against my fingertips as I played a chord in my dream. My mom, my dad, and my cat for some reason are there even though I didn't get that cat until long after I moved away. Dreams are strange like that sometimes when they muddy up the details of real life but still somehow feel right when you're dreaming. Ashton, Hanna, and Naomi are on the front lawn listening to me play those first chords and I smile. I squint as I stand and feel the blinding sun on my face, but I don't let it stop me from playing the song.

Everyone's eyes are on me and I step off the porch and just as I start to sing I'm ripped away to the sound of screeching tires just as I'm thrown forward and smash my face against the seat in front of me. The seat belt holds me safely in its grip despite the pain on my waist. I rock back and my head smacks against the seat and I'm *definitely* awake again.

I wince for a moment and undo my seat belt as I hold the back of my head.

"Stay here!" Aaron commands.

I open my eyes to more confusion. A pickup truck is blocking the road in front of us and three men in all black are approaching us with guns. They look like a swat team but move well enough to fool me. The driver sits with his hands up. Scott is cowering in the front seat and has dropped down low.

What the hell is happening?

Aaron gets out of the car and Harry gets out the other side.

I hear voices behind us. I turn back and an SUV similar to the one we're in is stopped close and blocking us in. Three more men, dressed just as imposing as the ones in front with big guns approach us. They surround us like a pack of wolves.

Before I can process what's happening I hear several gunshots from all directions. My tired body tenses up at each pop. Yelping sounds that I've never made before escape my mouth and I'm already crying.

What the fuck is happening?

I peek up and see the driver slumped forward on the steering wheel as the horn blares into the morning.

"Stay here," Jack says to me. I look over at him. As I try to focus on his face, I notice how bad I'm shaking. "Don't move." He opens the door and stays behind it like a barricade with a handgun aimed but he is shot several times in the back and I watch him collapse to the ground.

"No!" I scream. "Jack!"

I stare at his body as one of the men stands over him. Jack raises his arm to point the gun and another man kicks his hand and the gun skids across the road and one of them shoots Jack in the face. The gunshot makes me flinch but I don't scream. I don't speak. I can't speak. I'm not convinced this is happening. I need to wake up. I need to be in my villa and just not remember getting there. I need for none of this to be real.

I'm paralyzed by the fear, helpless as I watch with a dumb look on my face.

The door opens and an arm reaches in and grabs me, ripping me from my seat and I plummet to the pavement. The hard road violates my palms as I try to steady myself to get to my feet. I see Aaron lying on the ground, blood pooling around him where he lies still. I stare at his lifeless eyes in disbelief. Voices bark at me in another language and I don't understand them. I hear them repeating something as I try to get up and then I feel an oppressive boot in my back force me back onto the road.

The morning sun rests on my skin, only now it's not poetic, only blinding as I wrench my neck to look up. I fall in line. I can't win.

I don't know what is happening but I know that I'm just a trapped rabbit in a snake's den. These men have guns. I don't try to fight it.

I stay down.

The only movement comes from my sniffling and rattled nerves. I see Harry closest to me and I see Jack on the other side of the car as I look underneath.

A conversation is happening with a boot pressed into my back. Just enough pressure to remind me who is in charge and make it difficult to breathe. The voices get louder and go back and forth and then I feel the impact on the back of my head with something hard. My vision goes bright white as I'm struck and the voices disappear.

7

The pulsing blood rushes through my head. The pressure only brings pain and I feel like my head weighs a thousand pounds as I try to move.

I try to take a breath and it's hard. A deep breath warranting only a little air. Something is on my face. I feel the fabric tickling my nose and can't help but start to panic. I try to scream but I'm gagged with something. I move my mouth to speak and feel the sting on my cheeks of tape stretching and peeling. Is my mouth taped? The inside of my mouth feels dry against what I'm imagining is a bunched up cloth or something. Some sort of thick cloth. What even is this? I move my tongue around and it feels dry and scratchy instantly when I rub it against the gag.

As I peel open my eyes, I know something has been put over my head. I try to reach to take it off but my hands are bound together. I try to move them and feel the resistance and hardness of the metal along with the sound of clinking.

Handcuffs?

What do you want? I try to say, but it only comes out as muffled noises with no real distinction.

I'm ignored.

I feel myself sitting upright and feel the familiar humming of a car. The sounds of driving.

A conversation is happening in this car. There's a man beside me and he's talking to two men in front of me. They speak to one another in varying volumes and bounce back and forth between rough English and what I can only assume is Dutch. I'm not able to make out enough English to know what they're talking about. The offensive fragrance of cigarette smoke fills my nose with every desperate pull of air. Second-hand smoke is the least of my worries right now though, although I feel like somehow I can still taste the smoke despite my mouth being obstructed. My head is pounding. I sit still and try to pretend I wasn't just kidnapped in a foreign country.

Fuck, fuck, fuck, shit! Each gulp of air isn't that at all, it's only a slight inhale against big efforts through my nose. Everytime I move my hands and the short chain on these cuffs clink and rattle it feels more like an alarm while I try to remain calm and pretend my heart isn't racing—even though it is.

Why are you doing this? I ask, failing to get the words past the gag. The sounds I make as I try to speak are pathetic and embarrassing as I'm crying and feeling helpless during this drive. I wrestle with my bound hands and squeal, panicking after being ignored from my muffled words that die before they can be heard. Strong hands grab my arms and keep me from fighting. Instinctively I pull away and kick my legs only to feel the arms wrap around my body and squeeze me. The strength of this man beside me constricts my small frame and makes it so much harder to breathe—as if the gag wasn't already bad enough.

Two different voices are shouting at what I assume is me, likely telling me to stop, but I can't understand them, only feel them.

"You must stop, girl," the man squeezing me says, his voice gruff and raspy, and his rancid breath reeking of cigarettes and dirty water. The smell makes me want to throw up but the thought of me doing so only makes my chest pound harder while I imagine drowning in my own vomit.

I want to talk back but it's pointless. I continue kicking, the harder I'm squeezed the harder my legs kick the seat in front of me.

"Hey!" a voice in the seat I'm kicking grunts. "Hey!" he says even louder. He continues in another language as I feel someone grab my ankles.

I squirm in the seat and the man bear hugging me applies more pressure. "Be good girl. You no move, okay?"

I try to scream as my body tenses up. I fight to pull my legs away from the other man's clutches but I'm too vulnerable.

"Do it!" one of them says. I have this bag over my head and can't see anything.

"Girl . . . I tell you. Stop!"

"Don't hit her face, you damage the goods," the other man says.

What does that mean? During my struggle I feel something hard crack me on the side of the head. The bear hug loosens and I collapse into the door.

Suddenly the immediate pain is married to the blinding white I see for a moment and the disorienting feeling as I try to move with no real plan. Just desperation.

That fucking hurt.

Before I realize it, I'm practically sleeping, still fighting to keep my eyes open before I pass out.

I'm jostled awake to the feeling of being jerked forward by my arms as my feet are dragged against the ground. The throbbing in my head makes my skull feel like it's going to explode. I stand in place, the two men standing on each side of me holding my arms tight.

I hear the sound of a metal gate scraping against the floor and then clicking. My head feels heavy and makes it difficult to hold myself upright. For a moment I feel weightless, as if I'm sinking, and I can feel the floor humming beneath me. The scent of dust, some kind of oil, and bleach flood my nose despite my face being covered.

The metal scrapes against the floor again after we've come to an abrupt stop. One of the men quickly pulls me off the floor and hoists me over his shoulder. His muscle digs into my stomach as I'm carried and I feel the darkness closing in as I'm lulled into a slumber to their distant voices, even though they're within reach of me. My head jerks as I feel myself slipping out of wakefulness, but I fall away from the sounds and smells and pass out once again.

Water splashes my face and I jolt awake with a claustrophobic and suffocating feeling. I sit up and look around. The bag had been removed from my head, but the gag is still in my mouth. I look down at my hands—still bound—and notice the clean steel cuffs and the friendship bracelet sitting against the one. I take in my new environment. I'm in, like . . . a storage room or something. It smells like motor oil and cleaning chemicals, yet somehow dirty and dusty all at once. The area is not too unfamiliar. Shelving units like you might see in a stockroom line the wall across from me. Stacks of wooden pallets line the wall, staged behind me. I'm left to sit on a filthy wooden bench that makes me imagine the splinters it threatens me with at just a glance.

Two men sit on the bench with me while two men with rifles—dressed the same as the men who ambushed us—stand by the doorway, still and stoic. The water drips from my face. My hair slings wetness like it's spraying as I shake my head to get the tickling rivulets to fall off. I try to stand and one of the men next to me whips an arm in front of me—stiff—like a suggestion not to bother getting up.

"You sit now. Your turn coming," he says in poor English.

I do as I'm told, sure that I'm giving away my thoughts with my eyes as I look at the man and then the men at the door with the guns. I don't know where I am, even if I were to know it wouldn't matter, not with my hands bound and my mouth stuffed with whatever this is. It's difficult to sit here against my will and not wonder what I'm doing here.

Why was I taken?

Why were my friends and driver killed in front of me only to take me to this warehouse . . . dungeon . . . hideout place.

Why are men with guns posted up?

Why do I *need* to be gagged?

The longer we sit here in silence, the more anxious I become. I can't stop bouncing my legs.

I don't know how long we were here before they splashed me with water, but it's only been a few minutes since then and it feels like an eternity waiting for . . . whatever we're waiting for.

I listen to the sounds around me, hoping to hear something I recognize, but none of this is familiar. One of the men with a gun keeps sighing every so often as he adjusts his feet. He must feel really inconvenienced playing door guard. I'm sure it's much better than playing the captive singer.

While the large storage room may be silent, minus the occasional feet shuffling and heavy breathing from the men, I can hear what sounds like a voice coming out of a loudspeaker outside of the room. I'm not able to make out what is being said, only that there is a voice speaking. I focus on that sound and it stops for a moment, interrupted by . . . applause? That definitely sounds like an applauding crowd. If I'm familiar with anything, it's an audience clapping.

The thought of clapping only reminds me of my restraints. I try shuffling my hands with very little wiggle room and one of the men beside me looks over at me. His eyes and stone face say more than his words ever need to, so I stop despite the urge that begs to get my hands free. Even if I could get my hands free, what then? Overpower four men with two assault rifles? It's difficult not to imagine fighting my four security guards in a more playful setting. It's even hard not to break down after what happened before I was brought to this place. Just as I have that thought, I notice he has a pistol strapped to his hip. I turn to look at the other man whose face meets mine with a more disgusted look. I can't help but feel intimidated. Small . . . oh, and he also has a pistol strapped to his hip as well. Four fucking guns between the two of them!

I feel my face heating up as I get angry. I want to scream so bad, but the noise dies before it can escape my mouth. I'm seething when my attention is broken by the *knock knock knock* at the door. One of the armed guards opens the door and a man pops in and the two have an exchange in a language I don't understand.

The door shuts, and the man with the gun looks at the men beside me and gives a thumbs up as he opens the door and he and his other gun-wielding buddy lead the way through the metal door.

Each man beside me grabs one of my arms as they stand. "You come now. It's your turn, girl."

One man squeezes my arm tighter than the other and I want to struggle to not feel the stronger grip but I know it won't matter. These men are going to do whatever they're going to do to me. The thought terrifies me to my core as I wonder how bad things could get. I'm in a foreign country, I don't speak the language, and so far everything about this is very bad. I'm really wishing this were a really messed up practical joke or something right now. Maybe the ambush was staged. The guns were Hollywood props and the blood was fake and my boys were in on it. God, I hope someone jumps out and yells *gotcha* right now. I wouldn't even mind the camera in my face if this could just all be for a good laugh.

We walk through a hallway that's poorly lit and with each step, the voice from the speaker gets closer. I feel the cloth gag against my front teeth and imagine it being removed. Hoping that it might get removed just so I can speak. Or so I can simply breathe.

We turn into an open space and I can hear the familiar bustling of a crowd on the other side of a large blue curtain that hangs from the ceiling and drags along the floor. A stout curly-haired woman stands by the curtain and holds up her index finger to the men and says something to them.

One man lets me go and steps away to lean against the wall. The other man pulls me along. "Okay girl. You see there, yeah?" he asks, pointing to the floor.

I look down and see an X on the floor made of blue painter's tape. I can't exactly speak to him, so I look at him and try to speak with my eyes, like I forgot how to just nod. I can't imagine how I must look right now, but I can't worry about that.

"You. Stand here," he orders, pulling me onto the X and standing in front of me with a hand on each of my shoulders, keeping me still as I stand here staring at him. "You wait, girl. You be good girl, yeah?" he asks as he taps on the gun on his hip. He walks over and joins his friend along the wall and smiles at me, giving me the thumbs up. It feels almost sarcastic—all things considered. I stare at the large curtains as the voice comes back onto the speaker, now much more clear than when we were down the hall behind a closed metal door. Is this some sort of private party? Are they about to make me go on stage and sing? What in the actual fuck is going on?

"Friends . . . Fellow associates . . . Artists," the voice says. A male voice. Not American, but clear enough English to understand fluently. "To close off this evening's festivities, we have quite the treat for you all." His voice is animated. Charismatic like a key speaker, or expert salesmen. What does he mean by *artists*? Are there other artists here? What is actually happening right now? "You've seen lots of high value and high profile status pieces tonight. But . . . we wanted to close off the evening with something special. Something that is truly one of a kind. An absolute bonafide, certified headlining item. A centerpiece." I feel sweat trickling down my ears and neck, and every new word he says in that upbeat cadence feels like a performance. My skin feels cold and I shiver nervously at the thought of what insidious plans are behind that performance. "We've been at this for some years now and I can truthfully tell you that this may be the highest valued commodity we've ever had come through The Exhibit."

Exhibit? Is this some sort of art show? I hear the murmurs in the crowd on the other side of the curtain and I'm getting scared at whatever this is. Am I the high commodity item? What the fuck does that even mean?

I stare down at my feet and realize I'm standing on the X.

These curtains are about to open and I'm going to be on display to whoever is out there.

"For the final item up for bid this evening . . ." For bid? What does that mean? *For bid.* "The princess of . . . No! The *Queen* . . . of pop culture, easily the most recognizable face and name in—not only America, but the world—pop culture. This generation's greatest songwriter, and most influential celebrity in all aspects. More awards than we have time to list off and a talent that transcends music and live performing."

This introduction is incredible but I can't help but be rattled at the thought of what is waiting on the other side of this curtain. The compliments and highlights of my career being listed off feel like weight being added to my chest. One new compliment is just one more brick crushing me and making it harder to breathe. Harder to focus.

"Put your hands together and prepare to pick up your jaw from the floor as I am humbly grateful to bring to you . . . the one . . . the only . . ."

I see light spill onto the floor at my feet as it bleeds through the curtain.

"Phoebe . . . Fox!"

I see the stout woman out of the corner of my eye pull on a rope and the curtains spread apart revealing the man speaking on a stage as he smiles at me and claps. The crowd is revealed as the spotlight spills in and nearly blinds me. As I raise my restricted arms to cover my face I realize I am also revealed to them as well.

The crowd cheers, clapping and whistling. I can sense the surprise in the voices that are drowned out by the more excitable cheers and screams. This reaction isn't too far from the fans who are normally in attendance at my concerts. I'm unable to see any of their faces really as the lighting is all on the stage, focused on me.

I am truly the brightest star in the room right now and all eyes are on me as I stand here confused, and even more terrified.

"I just want to remind everyone here this evening, that the rules of the Cultural Art and Performance Exhibit—AKA CAPE—dictate that what happens in this auction house, stays in this auction house. You are not to discuss what you have seen or heard here tonight." The man paces the stage. He's well-dressed, in a powder-blue sports coat over a white dress shirt and yellow tie. Blue pants to match the jacket. "Of course, that is to be implied, but I just have to remind all members. Anyone who violates this simple rule will be terminated from the program . . ." He turns to the crowd with excellent comedic timing and a smirk. "And no one . . . wants that."

The crowd offers a laugh and the man with the microphone shuffles to the side of the stage. The light feels hot all of a sudden, shining brighter on me. I feel like I'm in a terrarium more than a stage. Maybe it's just the eyes that peruse my body and see my vulnerable and forced-to-stand-here state.

"How does one value the biggest superstar in the world?" he asks, looking over at me. His slimy eyes look me up and down. It's like I can feel them slithering up my body with his gaze. "Mmm mm *mm*, someone here tonight is going to win a total package and have," he turns to the crowd with a dramatic pause. "A *really* good time."

A few people laugh.

I am not one of them.

"Can we start the bidding at one million dollars?" he asks, going into a changed cadence with his voice. He has gone into that fast-talking auctioneer voice, but not quite as fast and funny. "Who wants to kick it off for us?"

One million dollars!? Holy shit! This is bad. While I cannot see faces, I can see shadows and silhouettes in the crowd. It looks like people are sitting at small tables like it's a comedy club or a lounge bar. I see at least a dozen hands shoot up holding sticks with small red lights on them.

"Oh, okay, we've got some interest, as expected. I *love* it! Let's see who wants to party with the gorgeous Phoebe Fox!" He steps to the edge of the stage, looking out at the crowd. "Do I have two million? Two million for the most-streamed-on-Spotify and Apple Music artist, Phoebe Fox."

Two lights lower down and click off.

"I am liking what I'm seeing here ladies and gentlemen. Can we get three million for Miss Fox, no?"

No one budges.

Under any other scenario I would feel flattered. Three million is so much money! Nothing good can come of this. I can't fight back the tears or hide the shaking in my knees. I don't think I've ever been so afraid in my life and the anxiety of whatever is coming next is only making it worse.

"Oh ho ho, I must say, I thought I was coming in a bit high with one million to start, but I can certainly see how wrong I was. Ladies and gentlemen, can we get five million for Phoebe Fox? Five million?"

He scans the room and two more lights lower and turn off.

"Wow, we have some incredible members here at the CAPE. I just want to remind you that the money from the winning bidder goes partially to keeping this place running but also goes into select funds and community projects in different programs around the world that support the arts and encourage the future generations of cultural expression. With that said, do we have," he stops to stare across the room. "Ten . . . million . . . dollars?"

Four lights lower and turn off. Four lights remain raised in the darkness. Holy fucking shit. There are four people out there willing to pay ten million dollars for me.

"Time to be bold here, boys and girls. Do we have . . . Twenty million dollars?" Two lights lower and disappear. Now only two remain.

Two red lights glowing in the darkness, like monster eyes peering at me, waiting to take me into the dark too.

"Twenty . . . five? Do we have twenty five million dollars for the beautiful Phoebe Fox?"

Ugh. The way he says my name feels dirty.

The two lights, the red beacons that watch me with hunger remain, hovering above faces that I can't see, but can't help but wonder if I would recognize.

"Thirty million. Do we have thirty million?"

The two lights remain. This has to be some sort of sick joke. Maybe all of this was part of a reality show that really wanted to go over the top. If the point was to fucking scare me, congrats, I am good and scared.

"Thirty five million?"

The lights do not waver. I'm beginning to wonder what these people think they're getting out of me.

"Wow. This is impressive. Miss Phoebe is drawing quite the bank roll tonight." The auctioneer paces to the other side of the stage. "Do we have," he lowers his voice, nearly to a whisper, like he's telling a secret that the entire audience is in on. "Fifty million dollars?"

I stare anxiously at the glowing red pair of eyes that watch me eagerly. Just as I get used to seeing them, one lowers down and turns off and is swallowed into the darkness of the room.

"Ladies and gentlemen, Phoebe Fox has just sold for fifty million dollars to the person with the last light remaining. I am also proud to tell you that you are now the record holder for the most money spent on one canvas here at the CAPE. We look forward to your installation and seeing how creative you get with your new clean canvas."

Canvas? What is that supposed to mean?

As I stare out into the crowd I feel hands grab my arms and it's my brooding captors from the storage room I woke up in. "You come now, girl."

I'm pulled away, my feet nearly tripping over each other as I try to figure out what just happened and what this all means. The curtain closes behind me as I pass through and we're walking through the hallways with the cold concrete walls again.

"Make sure if you've won an item tonight that you complete your transaction immediately," I hear the man on stage continuing as we walk away. "Make sure you're using a dark wallet to send cryptocurrency to complete your purchase."

We make the walk quickly down a hallway that is new to me. There are doors on both sides. We pass several as we head down this corridor and we stop. The doors are metal and look heavy. There are tiny windows to look through with metal screen fencing over them. One of the men pulls it open and the hinges whine in protest with every inch wider its pried open.

The man stands inside and turns to me and gestures with his arm out for me to come in. I hesitate, not knowing what might happen to me in this room if I go in.

"You go now, girl," the man holding my arm says. His voice isn't threatening at all so I look at him. His eyes look away from mine, almost like he's ashamed. "S'okay, girl. You go now."

I linger with my eyes on him. I want to speak but it isn't an option.

"Come," the other man says from the entryway to the room.

I feel my arm pulled as I'm dragged in from the hallway. I don't fight at first, not until I see what is waiting inside the room.

9

I'm pulled into the room and it has the aesthetic of a military bunker surrounded in concrete from wall to wall, floor to ceiling. Bleach fumes singe my nose as I'm greeted by the hospital-like smell of what seems like some third-world version of a medical exam room. I try resisting the hands grabbing me when I see the metal chair that's bolted to the floor along with the thick chain and shackle with the same treatment.

No! I try to scream in protest, but again . . . gagged, muffled, effectively silenced. My mumbling is ignored despite my efforts and hopes of my pleading to sneak past this obstruction in my mouth. The longer it's there the more I start to feel tape on my cheeks peeling slightly with the different facial expressions I make.

"Yes, yes, you come, you sit," he commands, manhandling me into the chair. The other man comes over and holds me down, making it difficult for me to squirm and fight. The man who has been the most talkative of the two slips the shackle around my ankle and I hear the lock click and immediately feel the weight of the chain pulling me into the ground. The longer I sit here, bound and gagged, the more it feels like the chain is pulling me into my grave. "You stay, girl. Now we wait."

Wait for what? I don't like this at all. Why am I chained up? Who just purchased me in a fucked up auction for fifty million? I need to get out of here and find help. But how?

I look around and see in the middle of the room is a flat metal table. A drain waits beneath it in the floor, waiting for whatever is to be rinsed away in here. That explains why it smells so artificially clean in here. They probably just hose this room down and spray chemicals all over the place. Why would they need to hose the room down though? My stomach turns at the thought of what seems obvious.

Beside the table is a cart with various tools on it and I don't need to be a genius to know that those aren't for a routine check-up. The picture is clear now and as my stomach twists and turns again I can feel it in my throat. Someone is planning to torture me or something. I see things that look sharp and other medical tools that I've seen on TV but I have no idea what they are. It takes everything in me to tune everything out and not retch.

Two overhead lamps light the room—poorly—and the silence is only broken by the hum from the bulbs. My two keepers stand quietly, only with the occasional shuffling of their feet. I adjust my own and the weighted chain drags against the floor and is accompanied by the sounds of metal touching. The noise is like a neon sign screaming, *Look at me!*

I don't know how long we've sat here. It feels like forever, but has probably only been ten or twenty minutes. Why does waiting for forever feel like waiting to die? My morbid question is interrupted by a knock at the door.

One of the men opens the door and pokes his head out. I'm unable to see who is on the other side, but I hear soft-spoken words being exchanged before the door is opened wider. The man at the door looks to our other friend, the more chatty of the two, and he snaps his fingers at him and points to me as he makes a sharp whistling sound.

The man hustles over and drops to a knee to undo my shackle. *What is happening?* I try to ask but he can't possibly know what I'm trying to say.

I hear the shackle drop against the floor and immediately feel relief from not having the chain holding me down. "We go now, we clean you up, yes?" He looks at me wearing a grin. The way he talks to me is patronizing, like how a parent might talk to a toddler who doesn't know that taking a bath is in their best interest. Fuck this guy.

He grabs my arm and pulls me to my feet aggressively, clearly warning me not to step out of line or things will go badly. I whimper, making noises that sound as pathetic as they feel. We walk through the door and pace along the hallway until we enter a room that seems a bit more familiar to me. The room is long and there are several rotating seats that line up along a long built-in countertop with mirrors. This room is much better lit than the previous one I was in. This feels more like a salon or make-up trailer.

I'm ushered in where a middle-aged woman gestures for me to have a seat. Her smile is perfect, with unrealistically white teeth. The kind of smile that seems genuine and friendly but completely out of place. "Please, come have a seat," she says, in a perfect American accent. I hesitate, I'm sure she can see my suspicion in my eyes as I study her, wondering where she's from. She taps the back of the seat with her hand, making the vinyl backing smack loud in the room. "Come come, we've gotta get you all cleaned up." I'm guessing New York . . . definitely northeast if I were betting, maybe Connecticut or Vermont. Philly. It doesn't matter, what matters is what does she want with me? Is she the person who just spent millions for me out there?

I look at the man holding my arm, the one with all of the words. He scrunches his face and nods at me, approving. "You, sit. It's good. She make nice."

His grip on my arm guides me to the chair where I take my time obeying. The urgency of my movements are really all I have control of, I guess. "There we are, good stuff," the woman says. "How are you doing tonight Phoebe?"

What? Is she serious? What kind of insane question is that!? Does she not see me or the situation at all? She can't be that oblivious, can she? I stare into my reflection ahead of me as I fall into the most comfortable seated position I can. I lock eyes with her in the mirror as she waits for my response.

"Hey, fellas, can we get this thing off her mouth so I can at least have a conversation with my girl here? Please?"

She asks them to remove my gag but it feels more like an order. One of the guys comes over and removes it. He rips tape off of my mouth and I feel every tiny hair I didn't realize was on my face come with it. Even though it hurts like hell, the relief of the cloth coming free makes that pain worth it.

I breathe in deep like I can't take in enough air, gulping whatever I can get. I bet I sound like I've been running a marathon.

"Poor girl. You must be thirsty," the woman says. She snaps at one of the men. "You. Make yourself useful and fetch Miss Fox a bottle of water. Please and thank *yooooou*." She walks around to stand in front of me and smiles at me, showing all her teeth. This would be unusual even if I *weren't* restrained and in a scary unfamiliar place. "Phoebe, girl," she says to me like we're close friends about to gossip. "You *have* to tell me," she starts as if I have all the tea while she lifts a box off the floor by the handle and sets it on the counter in front of the mirror. "What is it like to be a big ole superstar?"

I hesitate. Not intentionally. I stare at her—almost in disbelief that she could have this kind of conversation right now. My jaw hangs open. "Do you not see what's happening to me right now?" I ask, feeling the dry, gravelly anger as I raise my voice, lifting my hands to show her they're handcuffed. I notice the bruises starting to form around my wrists.

"Shoot! We've gotta get you out of those clothes and into something more . . . glamorous." She walks to the end of the room where a moving wardrobe on wheels sits with clothes on hangers. She shuffles through one to the next as the sound of the hanger hooks scrape across the metal bar they cling to.

Scccccrape.

Scrape.

Scrape.

Scccccrape.

"Your new artist was *very* insistent that you wear this in particular," she says, showing off a two piece outfit, very similar to something I've worn on stage recently. "If they pay good money for a canvas it's my job to accommodate them before they come to their studio."

"What do you mean by *new artist*?" I ask. She's talking like I'm a record label executive or something.

"Well," she says, ignoring me while looking at the guards with eyes that say, *What are you waiting for?* "Get to it. Grab the scissors and let's get her dressed. Quickly now. Chop chop!"

The two burly men stand me up, grabbing my arms again. "What are you doing!?" I ask after feeling hands tugging on my pants and pulling them off aggressively. Threads popping and tearing as my entire body tenses up. I feel like a little girl's doll and she's changing my clothes, using all this muscle to do so.

"Be still, girl. I no want to cut you," the one man says as he flashes a pair of scissors, opening and closing them to the same rhythm he wiggles his eyebrows. "I no hurt you, girl."

I feel my chest tighten at the sight of them.

"Hold out your hands," he says, showing me a small key like it's a special treat. I hold out my hands and he makes quick work of removing the cuffs. I massage the redness and bruising from where they were on so tight and pressing into my skin.

The woman walks over to me and looks at my wrists. I flinch against her thumb pressing into the bruises. "I'm sorry honey. I need to take this though." She slips the friendship bracelet off my wrist where it rolled up my arm.

Strong enough.

I don't feel strong right now. I feel anything but strong.

"Let's get her dressed, boys," she says, clapping twice as she walks away, twirling the beaded bracelet on her finger. "If she tries to fight you, try to only break a finger or two. No blows to the head or bullet wounds please. They leave a terrible mess and I don't feel like explaining what happened."

"Stop . . . stop it!" I cry out as he holds the scissors away from me. The other man pulls my pants down with authority. I step out of them to stop the violent jerking and pulling. He tosses them aside.

Fear grips my voice and my bones rattle like the room is cold, even if it's not. Everything is happening to me so fast. I feel my shirt being tugged and the scissors gliding through the fabric like wrapping paper as I stand here frozen, keeping my feet close together and my front covered as the shirt comes off. I feel my bra unlatched in the back and it makes me start to cry not knowing what's about to happen, but thinking about what *might* happen. Scissors cut the straps and I feel my bra come off with no fight. It's tossed aside near my pants and shredded shirt. The woman tosses the bracelet on top of the pile of clothes like common waste.

My bottom lip trembles and I can't control the quiet noises that come from my mouth. It's like I'm vibrating in place. I feel fingers slip into my panties on the outside of my hip and I close my eyes and a whimper escapes me. A sound I've never made before, like a scared animal more than a person.

"That's enough," the woman says. "She can keep her panties."

My cheeks tingle as chills run along my body with the audible sigh of relief as I open my eyes and stare at the woman. She walks behind me. "Move," she says, shooing the men back. "Raise your arms up for me."

"What . . . what are you going to do to me?"

She holds up the yellow corset, with sequins shimmering like gemstones. "I'm just getting you dressed. We've gotta get you ready." I do as she says and raise my arms. My bare breasts are exposed, leaving me feeling vulnerable.

"Ready for what?"

She stands behind me, reaching around to fasten the corset onto me. I feel her hands, gentle as they cup my breasts, while she adjusts me into the top. She tightens it, causing me to gasp and stand upright. "Perfect. You look stunning, Phoebe. You truly are a superstar . . . just look at you." She rests her chin on my left shoulder and stares at me in the mirror with doe eyes. The way a mother looks at her daughter before sending her off to prom. She breaks away and stands in front of me with the matching skirt, yellow with the sequins held up to me. "Let's get you into this."

She squats down, holding the skirt open in a way for me to step into it. One foot at a time I step in and she pulls it up and goes back behind me to zip it up. It feels uncomfortable, unlike the version of this I wore for my shows, but I have to admit, it's a pretty good replica outfit.

"Oh, I almost forgot!" she says, prancing over to grab something. She rushes back over with a pair of white boots. "These too! Here, sit down, I'll help you get them on." I sit in the chair and she begins to slide the long boots on. They go just below my knees and have several straps along the leg that make me look like a wrestler almost. Or a cheerleader. "Perfect!" she says as she stands back up and looks at me. "They fit! I was worried they might not!"

I look down at the clean white boots. "What are you going to do with me?"

She turns to the counter, back to the box with the handle and opens it, revealing an assortment of makeup items and lays out a rolled up brush set then lets it unfurl along the length of the counterspace. "Oh, pretty girl. Don't you mind that right now. I'll get you out of here in a jiff."

"What is this place?" I ask with an edge to my words.

She holds two bottles of foundation up to my face, one on each side. Is she seriously checking my complexion right now? "Well this is The Exhibit, Miss Fox. Did no one tell you when you got here?"

"I guess they forgot that part when they knocked me out in the car."

She turns to grab another bottle and holds it up to my face and twists her lips like she's perplexed. "Hmmm, I think this shade will work," she says to herself.

"Please," I start to beg. "You have to get me out of here." I'm disgusted at how weak I sound now from when I was just seething at her, but I can't help myself from trying.

"You know," she starts, as she uses a wet wipe on my face. "I never used to listen to your music." She wipes around my chin and under my nose. This feels like I'm backstage before a concert . . . minus the armed men and panic attack I'm having. "To be honest, I never really cared for you."

"Please," I say, lowering my voice to almost a whisper.

"Shh, shh, shhhh," she says in a low and calming voice. She continues to wipe my face with another wipe, ignoring my pleading. "Not until my daughter started playing your songs." She tosses the wipe onto the floor and unscrews the cap to the foundation bottle. She dips the applicator several times before she begins to apply it to my face. "She plays your music all of the time. Hell . . . even my nieces are obsessed with you now."

I move my face around, getting annoyed that she isn't answering me. "Why am I here? Why is this happening to me!?"

"After hearing that song of yours, *Problem,* on repeat, over and over," she continues. It's like I'm talking to the wall. What am I supposed to do here? "I found it stuck in my head when my girls weren't around. I think I softened up and became a fan of you at some point. It's so strange how over time I found myself singing along in the car with my little girl."

Okay, I need to approach this differently. She's a mother, so maybe that's the right move. "What's your little girl's name?"

She uses a beauty blender to set the makeup in. "Heather is my baby girl."

"If you help me get out of here, I can come visit Heather," I offer. "I can really make her day. You'd be the coolest mom . . . if you made that happen." I'm feeling desperate here, really reaching now. "You could tell her we're really good friends."

"I think it's great that she has someone like you to look up to," she pats my face with the beauty blender. "A strong empowered female role model."

"Did you hear what I just said?" How could she not react to that? "I can give her—I can give Heather the best fan experience anyone has ever had."

She continues to touch my face and the brush tickles my cheeks. "When I was a kid I remember my daddy being concerned about me listening to musicians who weren't the best of role models so I guess it's good that she listens to you rather than–"

"Let me the fuck out of here!" I scream, my voice shrieking enough to cause her to jump. She steps back with a coy smile and a hand on her chest.

"Well sheesh, fine," she looks around the room with big-eyed stares at the two men, with a look that suggests I'm somehow being unreasonable. "You win, Phoebe. We're done here. All cleaned up." She turns to put her makeup supplies back in the container. I lock eyes with her in the mirror as I watch her smile and light tone disintegrate. "Gentlemen, take her away."

I watch her grab her kit and walk away. "No! . . . No! . . . You've got to help me!"

Just as I scream and stand up, I feel a firm hand on each of my arms and a hand covers my mouth. The man looks into my eyes through the reflection of the mirror. "You want gag? Or you want be quiet?"

My heart rate picks up and I say nothing. I don't want the gag again.

"Thassa good girl," he says. "Come. We go back."

The quiet one grabs my hands while the talkative one puts on a thick black zip tie, securing it tight to my wrists. I really hoped that was it for the restraints. They pull me toward the door, guiding me. "Where are we going?"

The series of boots clomping along the floor are foreboding in the hallways. "Back to studio. You clean now. You meet new owner."

Studio? Does he mean that cold room I was in before? Owner? What the fuck is going on here?

"Who is my owner?" I ask, looking at the quiet one. He ignores me completely as we walk. I turn to the more talkative one. "Who is my owner?"

"Your owner is artist at Exhibit."

The trip back to the room feels quick, probably because I want it to take forever. The forever like earlier when time seemed to be frozen. They open the door and let me in where I'm told to have a seat. I'm hesitant to comply but my choices feel non-existent—all things considered. The shackle is closed around my ankle and the chain makes me imagine my feet are like rocks under the earth as I feel my weight sink into the floor. I think of those old gangster movies my dad would watch. People tossed over a bridge into water with weights chained to their feet, ensuring they sink deeper and deeper and never leave. The two men leave and the door is pulled shut and I feel like the weights are pulling me through dark water. The sound the door makes as it's sealed shut feels more like sealing my fate, uncertain of whatever awaits me the next time it opens.

10

D read lingers in the air as I study my surroundings. I look around for cameras, wondering if I'm being watched. I don't see any . . . not in here at least. The overhead lighting crawls through the reflective sequins on my new out-of-place outfit and keeps catching my attention. Bright yellow sitting against a dull and dreary backdrop. My eyes keep shooting to the drain on the floor, like it's taunting me with a question I'm not ready to be answered. My clean white boots practically glowing against the filthy and heavy chain attached to the shackle keeping me here. My eyes keep finding the door, wondering what's waiting for me the next time it opens.

The room is silent aside from my own heart beating.

Who is my *artist*?

Are they on their way now?

What exactly am I waiting for?

Is this part of some sort of initiation for someone? Who has that kind of money to spend that I know? It's tough to think of anyone who would be in a place like this. I don't even know what this is exactly, but I know these people are up to no good. I've made a lot of enemies over the years, but who is willing to spend that much to do whatever they're gonna do?

Crazy fans are a possibility, but the amount of money seems absurd. It would have to be someone with significant status. Who would have that sort of money and be willing to risk it all? Surely they have more money to spend than what they just paid.

I move my foot in a circle to feel the chain resisting to amuse myself. Anything to not think about what's next. There's a bug of some sort here with me. I watch it buzzing, zipping around one of the lights in the ceiling. The bug's body taps as it repeatedly collides with the light.

Tink.

Tink.

Tink.

I'm sure at least ten minutes have passed while I've watched this bug. I'm imagining how crazy I'd have to be if the bug were to suddenly speak to me, and how much crazier I'd be if I spoke back. I stare at the bug crawling along the light bulb and I wonder what Aaron or Jack would do in this situation.

Oh fuck. Aaron, Jack, Harry, and Scott, all gone because of me. My chin falls into my chest as I weep. The sobs echoing as the fly taps against the bulb again.

Tink.

Tink.

My guards—my friends—my brothers . . . They have families who have no idea what happened. This shouldn't have happened. I feel sick thinking about what their loved ones are going to say to me if they ever get the chance. They're going to be absolutely destroyed.

My nose runs as the tears fall, thinking about how they were paid to protect me and died doing it.

Tink.

Tink.

I know that's what they signed up for and that it was always a possibility, but damn it feels like my heart is in a vice grip being tightened as I think about them.

I can still hear the glass hitting the road and feel the car spinning when I close my eyes.

I feel crazy just thinking this and I revert back to quietly panicking in my mind. My instincts are screaming at me to run as I imagine the worst possible scenarios, but I can't leave. The more I think about it the harder it is to breathe. The air around me is frigid against my bare skin and my stomach twists and twists. I flex my arms while making fists, straining my muscles against the zip tie to only feel the unforgiving plastic digging more into my skin. I feel the redness on my wrists as I struggle, wishing like hell the zip tie would come apart. I think about how Aaron just taught me how to break a zip tie in this exact situation not long ago. I can probably break free, but what then? I'm still chained to the floor. I don't know how many people are walking around with guns. I don't even know where I am. The thought enters my mind of breaking the zip tie and something worse being done to me when they come in here. Would they restrain me better, making it harder to be free? I don't want to be more restricted so I shouldn't. Not yet.

Tink.

Tink.

The silence of the room aside from that bug tapping the light becomes overwhelming as my thoughts race and I fail to control a singular thought for more than a moment. That's when I hear a man's voice screaming from through the wall behind me.

"Hello!?" I cry out.

The scream, there it is again, begging to be heard through the concrete walls that muffle the voice. I stand and face the wall behind the chair and just stare at it, like I'm waiting for the cold and gray cement to speak. The zip tie digs into my wrists more and more as I move my hands, leaving bruises like stains. The chain drags along the floor, only allowing me a very short distance to move. The wall looms over me, foreboding as I listen close to try and hear another scream, desperate to decipher words. Would I even understand them if they were saying anything? Will that be me soon? That scream is only agony to my ears, but waiting for it to sound again is agony in my mind.

Time passes slowly as my anxiety reaches new peaks. I pace along the pale concrete floor just to listen to the chain jingle, like a toddler playing music. There it is again . . . that scream from the other side of the wall. I think it's a man's voice. It's hard to tell. Just as I press my ear to the chill of the wall, the door opens, startling me before I hear the footsteps that follow. Footsteps that don't align with the heavy boots of the two men who have *so kindly* escorted me from place to place.

"Thank you, gentlemen," a man says with a stern and authoritative, familiar voice. "That'll be all. I'll holler if I need you."

Oh fuck . . . this isn't good. An older man, Wayne Silverman, just waltzed into this cement tomb in a black power suit and a stride that suggests he's here for business. My jaw would be on the floor right now if I weren't clenching my teeth so hard.

Wayne Silverman is a powerhouse in the music industry with an eye for talent as a record executive with deep pockets from decades of managing many top stars. Not only is Wayne a mean business man with unethical practices and a reputation for undercutting others, but he's also my professional and personal nemesis if there ever was one. Wayne is a dirty old man and no stranger to controversy and shady people.

"Hello there, Phoebe." He unbuttons the cuff on his sleeve as he makes his way toward me. I stand frozen and unable to speak. His dark eyes and box-dyed black slicked back hair stare into me. His face hardened. "What's the matter?" he asks as he begins unbuttoning the other cuff. "You look like you've seen a ghost." He stands in front of me, looking me up and down with a cocky smirk that I want to smack off his too-tanned wrinkled face so bad.

Early in my career, this smug son of a bitch basically strong-armed my previous manager into selling him the rights to all of my music without even giving me a chance to buy it myself. Who does that?

He walks over to the metal table that sits over the drain in the floor as he's unbuttoning his expensive-looking suit. "Yeah, that's the look of someone scared of ghosts," he says in his raspy voice.

He's right though. It is like seeing a ghost. After our public spat that got blown way out of proportion and things were said in interviews, something out of my control happened. My fans stepped up and used their voices and their money to basically boy-cott Wayne. Things got a little out of hand with some of the fans who sent death threats to him and his family. Wayne Silverman and other artists he managed at the time did well to make my life a living hell. So much so that I had to disappear and find myself again. I wish things could have been handled better, but at the time I felt betrayed by people in charge of my passion and at the end of it all I was only left with my voice.

"From the shallowest grave hidden in the darkest shadows of the earth, I'm here now, Phoebe." He pulls himself away from his suit jacket and folds it with care before laying it on the surface of the table after brushing it off with his hand.

"What do you want, Wayne?" I ask, my words laced with fire that slips past my teeth.

He grins as he turns to face me, leaning back against the table. He loosens the tie at his neck. "Well isn't it obvious? It's you I want."

Why am I not surprised that this scumbag Wayne Silverman is the winning bidder?

"You thought you'd seen the last of me, but here I am."

"What do you want with me? Haven't we done enough?"

"Perhaps you feel we've done enough, sure. But isn't that easy to think from your throne in the clouds?"

"What are you talking about?"

"You know exactly what I'm talking about you little twat!" he growls, more of an impulse than a response. I sense his rage from how his words rattle his chest and echo in this room. He walks toward me slowly pulling his tie off completely and unbuttoning the top button of his white dress shirt. "You know it was really easy for you after all of it. Sure, I walked away with the rights to your music, but the public skinned me alive. I got dragged through the mud. My name . . . my reputation . . . everywhere for the world to see. Nobody wants to work with me. Business deals fell through. My grandkids asking why I was so mean to little Miss Phoebe fucking Fox."

"Your reputation was shit before you met me and you know it!"

"Maybe, but the difference is that I was managing the biggest talents in the music industry before. Now . . . I'm staying out of the spotlight and too rich to give a damn."

"So why do you want me?"

"I really just wanted a moment to talk is all. I think your story is a good one, after stepping back and taking a moment to reflect. Truly, I mean that. You went up against the record label machine and lost but you weren't too beaten to burn it to the ground on your way out. I know you won't believe me when I say this but, I respect the hell out of you Phoebe. This is coming from a white-collar cutthroat from the Bronx."

I stand afraid of whatever he is up to. I've never trusted him, ever, and the cockiness behind his words feel like a lion clamping its jaws around my neck. Realizing how vulnerable I am with my hands bound and my ankle chained I feel the pit in my stomach swallowing itself and it makes my body spasm. "Do you ever stop talking? Just get on with it already."

"You're not as polite as I remember." He chews on the inside of his cheek and I can see him moving his tongue around the inside of his mouth with a look of disgust on his face as his eyes shoot needles through me. The hair on my neck raises and I can feel the cool air of the room as he stands in front of me. His cologne violates my senses. "You found a way to rebuild yourself. You record songs you've already sung and now you're doing a mega tour of all of the tours you've already toured." He claps. "Bravo Miss Fox. Bra-fucking-vo! You found a way to exploit your fans. You steal allowances from thirteen-year-old girls who look to you as a role model by selling them over-priced merchandise. Do you sleep better at night by calling it 'limited edition'? You've somehow managed to make yourself a symbol of inspiration for what taking back control looks like for women around the world. You outsmarted standard business practices and called it fighting misogyny. And you did it all after dragging my name through the mud.

"You see, I don't come around much anymore. I've been a member of The Exhibit for the last few decades . . . being one of the biggest players in the game, it comes with perks like this place. But, it wasn't until a little bird told me that Miss Phoebe Fox was going to be the premiere item of the night for The Exhibit. All of that hostility and hate for you that I once let go of came rushing back like a thousand waves crashing under a raging storm. It's poetic that you would be handed to me on a platter like this. What better way to teach you a lesson?"

"How does this teach me anything other than you somehow being an even bigger asshole?" I say, acting stronger than I'm feeling.

He steps closer to me, snickering. "There is no amount of money I wouldn't have paid tonight to have this opportunity to put an end to the Phoebe Fox era." He raises his hand to my chin and makes me face him. I jerk away and his hand wraps around my jaw as he squeezes. His other hand holds my bound wrists causing the zip tie to dig into my already bruised skin even more.

He shoves me into the chair as the back of my head slams against the backrest. The weight of his strength keeps me afraid and unable to retaliate. My instinct is to kick him with my free leg but his knee is pressed hard into my thigh rendering me unable to fight at all. His nostrils flare as his tone softens but his words sharpen.

"You should take comfort knowing that when you're gone, your fans will only miss you for a moment, and soon another pretty young whore will come into the spotlight . . . and your fans will move onto the next big thing. Girls only like shiny things and when you're done here, there won't be any shine left."

His breath stings my face and the hate spews like acid from his lips. My body is tense and I'm defenseless. My castle walls have crumbled and there is nothing to protect me. I think of what giving up might look like, but even worse what it might feel like. Then, I'm reminded of how close he is to me. How I can feel his disdain toward me. I can feel the sincerity in his voice that he means what he says. His closeness makes things more uncomfortable after he calls me a whore and I realize he could treat me like one and I wouldn't be able to stop him. He stares at me like a predator playing with their food. I feel his closeness from his hot breath on my face and the thickness of his cologne. Imagining what he might do terrifies me. Is this new nightmare about to take center stage?

Every exhale comes out of his nose and is accompanied by a growling noise in his throat as his eyes pick me apart. He looks me up and down and I shiver against his gaze. "You know, Phoebe . . . the thing about pop stars is . . . they get big . . . really big." My heart jumps inside my chest when I see his eyes land on my breasts as he says that. "Their heads fill up with so much air. They get bigger . . ." He brings his face closer to mine, "and bigger," he whispers, "until eventually . . . the pop star . . . goes," he lets me go and backs off me. "POP!" he yells, loud enough to shake me to my core.

My chest tightens.

I can't keep from crying.

I struggle to catch my breath.

I don't know how I'm not out of tears by now.

He walks over to grab his suit jacket, buttoning the top button of his shirt again. "You know, I used to come here and drop a few thousand dollars and have my way with a person or two, but nowadays I'm not a fan of getting my hands dirty." Wayne pulls on his suit jacket and goes to the door to leave as I watch him, paralyzed with fear from the chair. He knocks on the heavy door with a cheerful pattern. "My hands are clean," he says calmly as the door opens. "But my daughter has been dying to finally meet you," he sneers as he walks out of the room and I'm left to wonder who his daughter is.

The Rise of Phoebe Fox - Part 2

Phoebe Fox would become a regular for the Grand Ole Opry for the next few years, before taking on bigger showcases around town as she built up her esteem.

Martha Fox

Word was getting around about this pretty young
  girl and her talent was starting to do a lot of
the heavy lifting I guess. We started getting calls
from smaller venues around town to have her audition
for showcases and make appearances. A lot of these
places were just bars on the strip, but we weren't
eager to turn down a good stage. Phoebe wanted to
  play all of the shows she could. She started to
              become obsessed with it.

[A young blonde woman in a white blouse and light
gray dress pants steps into frame in a different
room. There is a bookshelf out of focus in the
background as she takes a seat, positioned to the
right side of the screen. On the lower left of the
screen a name is displayed. Hanna Chance, Former
dancer, Longtime friend.]

Hanna Chance

I think she was about sixteen, seventeen, she
invited me out to one of the bars on Broadway to
watch her do lead vocals for another band. She was
                incredible.

Martha Fox
You could see at that time, she was a little girl
in the malls, but in the bars she was a little..
.out of place, at first. I would always be there
with her to make sure she was safe and dealing with
favorable people.

Hanna Chance
A lot of the bars she would work at were kind of
sketchy.

Phoebe Fox
[Smiling through an awkward stare away from the
camera]
Yeah, some of those places looked better in the
photos. Mom made a lot of phone calls to set up
those shows and all I wanted to do was sing. So,
a gig was a gig at the end of the day no matter
how sticky the floors or how filthy the bathrooms
were.

Hanna Chance
She'd have to learn songs for these cover bands
where she was only playing with them for the weekend
or sometimes just one night, but there were times
when some of those guys—those fully grown men—got
a little too...comfortable.

*Phoebe was still a child while being the focal
point on stages for adults in lively environments
on weekends. Many people would come out to party*

while she sang and there were plenty of times that alcohol played a part for some in attendance who were not quite fans of her.

Hanna Chance

Phoebe was always real pretty but as she started to find her groove on stage and really become a performer, she also started dressing more extravagantly. More colors and pageantry. It was a country crowd most nights but some nights she would end up sticking out like a black sheep.

Martha Fox

She was starting to blossom into a young woman. She was getting more comfortable with who she was becoming. Her body was developing, but something about it ...something about that point in her journey, just never felt like my baby girl.

[An old home video plays of Phoebe on a stage where the audience is within arm's reach of her. She is in a silver one-piece dress with black boots. She sings a country song while the band plays until the music stops and the audience is booing. Phoebe stands there, looking around like she's waiting for directions from someone just before a bottle flies toward the stage, barely missing her as she flinches. The drummer comes to the front of the stage to shield her while the bass player hops down and a fight breaks out that only makes a rowdy crowd even more difficult to manage.]

Hanna Chance
That night was crazy. That was actually the first
time I ever came with her and her mom.

Interviewer
Did you go often after?

Hanna Chance
. . . I went a few more times, yeah.

Martha Fox
Drunks would always start heckling her. I'd hear
some men say the most awful things to her, or to
people around them in private about her.

Interviewer
What sort of things?

Martha Fox
You know, like how she's dressed. They would call
her names.

Phoebe Fox
If I had a penny for every time a complete
stranger called me a slut . . . or a whore .
[Phoebe shakes her head as she crosses her arms]
Well, I wouldn't need to sing songs or tour.

Martha Fox
All sorts of crude things. A lot of them didn't know
she was a minor. It was really hard for me to bite
my tongue at times.

Hanna Chance
Men would just objectify her. Not all men . . . but
I guess the *boys*.

Interviewer
How did you feel seeing that?

Hanna Chance
Oh, that's my bestie. It would piss me off. Her mama
would let a lot of the talk slide but it was when
people tried to put their hands on her or cheap
promoters tried to treat her like a child.

Martha Fox
After about three or four months of that I could
tell she was over the bars.

Phoebe Fox
I met a lot of good people in those days. But I also
met a lot of shady characters. Lots of guys telling
me what they think I want to hear.

Interviewer
Like what?

Phoebe Fox
[Audible laughter]
All *kinds* of things . . . I've had so many guys
walk up to me and hit me with *Hey beautiful* or
what are you doing later? Or *can I get a hug?*
It's just cringy to me now.

Hanna Chance
I think she knew she wasn't built for that scene.
She was bigger than bars. She just needed to
find the right audience and the right stage. She
needed to do her, and be her authentic self.

*The writing was on the wall for Phoebe's time in
small bars on the Nashville strip. It wouldn't
be long before a catalyst changed everything.*

Martha Fox
Phoebe had a bad taste in her mouth one night in
particular. She had a great show but when I met
her backstage afterward she seemed disappointed.
She was sulking on a barstool in the hallway. I
asked her what was wrong and she told me that all
the guys in the band got paid more than her. She
was undercut by the bar owner.

Hanna Chance
Oh Mama Fox doesn't play when it comes to her baby.
I've seen her go at grown men and get in their face
before, she can be scary if she needs to be. That's

a sweet woman. But that night, that was a feisty
woman.

Phoebe Fox

I sort of accepted early on that I probably wasn't
going to get paid too well, but by that point, I was
really starting to discover what kind of performer
I am. I was the face of these bar bands and I'm not
stupid . . . I know what people wanted to see, I
heard the comments and things people would say.

Martha Fox

Well, I'm her manager, but I'm her mom first and
I'll give it to you straight. I was red hot that
night.

Phoebe Fox

I was just kind of . . . numb. I was only seventeen
but even then, I had put in so much work up to
that point and it was just starting to feel like a
pursuit that may be for nothing.

*Phoebe understood what it was to cut her teeth
in the business, but was only just learning about
preferential treatment. Especially between men and
women.*

*Martha watched her daughter after that show, de-
feated, and it was the last straw for Martha.*

Martha Fox
I walked right up to the bar owner and asked him
what the hell was going on.
[audible scoff]
You pay those guys double what you pay my daughter?
The lead singer and the guitar player? Really?

Hanna Chance
Oh yeah, I heard about this one. I heard this one
was really really bad.

Martha Fox
This guy tells me, 'Look sweetheart, I'm gonna keep
it real with ya, women don't make it in this town.'
I say, 'Why? Because they can't make decent money
like the fellas do?' We go back and forth for a
minute and I can feel my blood boiling and I'm
starting to raise my voice. Phoebe is grabbing me
and trying to pull me away and I'm already seeing
red.

Phoebe Fox
I was scared. My mom is probably the sweetest person
you could ever meet and we're two women in a honky
tonk bar. I remember thinking I don't care about
the money, come on mama forget about it, let's just
go.

Martha Fox
He says, 'Women don't make money in these bars yada
yada yada,' or whatever. I tell him that it's his
bar and he has the choice to do what's right. He

tells me that maybe if she shook her ass up the
street at one of the other clubs she could make more
money. He told me sex sells and winked at her.

Phoebe Fox
[Shaking her head with her eyebrows raised and eyes
wide] Yeah, he winked at me like a creepy uncle.
It was gross. What's worse is that kind of stuff
happens all the time in those places. But my mom
saw that and she wasn't such a sweet woman anymore.
She became someone else when she saw that.

Martha Fox
I lose my cool and I smack the liquor off his breath.
Phoebe is tugging on me and telling me to come on
and forget about it. I'm yelling at this scumbag
that she's just a minor and telling him where he
can stick the other half of the money he owes her.
It was a bad night.

Interviewer
Have you ever heard or seen Martha lose it before?

Hanna Chance
Nope. She is one of the sweetest people I've ever
met. I don't think I've even heard her swear before.

Martha Fox
Phoebe told me in the car on the way home that night
she was done with the bars.

Feeling beaten down by the spotlights and bar scene at just seventeen, Phoebe was ready for a change. She knew if she was going to be a star that she needed to pivot. Nashville was a town for dreamers and everyone was there chasing the same one. She knew that to stand out would mean doing something new.

Hanna Chance

After the bars and small clubs, I remember we were hanging out one night at her house and she told me that she thinks she wants to make a record.

Interviewer

She hadn't recorded anything up to that point?

Hanna Chance

No. Just the live gigs and cover songs really. But that night she played me some stuff in her living room that she had been working on. She pulled out a stack of spiral notebooks and I could see it. I knew she had a talent, I did. There was something about that moment though, I could see her hunger and passion. She played me songs that she wrote and I was an audience of one all night.

[A home video plays of Phoebe playing guitar in the living room, walking around strumming and singing as she smiles into the camera.]

Hanna Chance
She would sing a couple lines, strumming on her
guitar, and then stop to tell me other ideas she
had for the song in the studio. She clearly had an
ear for music beyond my comprehension. And yes, she
sounded amazing even then.

It was time to leave the small stage behind.

It was time for her to stand out.

It was time to let her voice roar and be heard.

It was time to make a record.

11

Wayne leaves and as the door shuts behind him I break down. I pour my face into my knees, curling myself into a ball, weeping as I find myself seated on the floor. Weeping becomes wailing. "Let me out of here! God! Help me!" I scream, begging for anyone to hear my desperate plea. My voice carries strong but only returns to me like it's trapped too.

My heart pounds and I can feel it in my face. My sniffling being the only thing disrupting the silence for several minutes before I hear the screaming again, coming from the wall behind me. A man's voice rings through the thick wall, just noticeable enough to keep me quiet so I can focus on what I'm hearing. The agony in his voice is apparent, and now the screams are more frequent. Unable to escape the screaming that makes me cringe—even muffled through those walls—I try to bury my head between my knees from the floor.

That does little to nothing to keep that distant screaming away. My eyes pry open at what sounds like the hum of a powertool. The screeching sound sings along with a chorus of screams. Now the once muffled sound is all I can focus on. Who is over there?

I can hear the pitch of the tool screeching change like an indictment to my ears. It's probably cutting through something and all I'm imagining is someone being tortured next door. Blood spilling from a removed limb onto the floor where it eventually leads to a drain—just like the one in this room. I feel a lump in my throat and my cheeks tighten thinking that I might be screaming next as the stale air around me chills against my skin.

Just as the buzzing of the tool ceases—even though the screaming is only growing more desperate—the door to this room opens once more. The heaviness of it whines through the hinges as a woman walks in.

White boots, familiar.

Yellow sequin skirt that shimmers with each step, like the one I'm wearing.

And a yellow corset, exactly like this one. The one so generously picked out for me.

Oh fuck . . . that's Aimee! My social-media-made-famous impersonator @itsjustaimee13 on Instagram and TikTok. This girl has been a megafan for years. If there were a list of red flags with fans or possible stalkers, she is definitely on the list. She's made money on making public appearances just for how spot on she is with my look. It's unsettling how much she really does look like me. But, to dye and style your hair, get facial reconstruction surgeries, and build your whole personality around someone else is just . . . kind of sick.

As she comes in, she's carrying a large duffle bag and she slings it onto the table, where it lands with a thud. She looks right at me, fanning herself with her hand wearing a smile on her face that is difficult to look at without feeling like I'm staring at a twin I do not have. "Hi Phoebe! Oh. Em. Gee. I'm so happy to *finally* meet you!"

She bounces up and down as she offers small giddy claps. Her bubbly personality is all the more frightening considering my predicament. My blood boils and I feel the heat in my face as I come to the realization. "Wayne Silverman is your fucking father!?" I ask through a look of disgust I'm unable to fake.

Aimee's face tightens over clenched teeth. "Yeaaaah," she starts, dragging out the word. "I don't like to tell people he is, buuuut . . . it's true."

"Was this all so you could meet me? What is all this, Aimee?" I ask, showing her the chain around my ankle and clean white knee-high boots.

"This isn't what you think, Phoebe. But now that you mention it," she unzips the duffle bag and flips open the top flap. I'm unable to see what's inside. "I've been trying so hard to meet you. You're a tough cookie to track down," she says through a laugh. "I've tried messaging you on Instagram, YouTube, I've flown around the world to try and catch a meet and greet with you and you don't even reply to my messages." Aimee rests her palms against the lip of the table with a defeated look on her face. "I know this seems like a dramatic way to get that matching selfie with my *favorite* person on the planet, but what's a girl to do?"

Her energy feels like that of a little girl. There is an unpredictability to her that makes me want to crawl out of my skin. She's right though. She has messaged me numerous times, tagged me in so many selfies and videos, and I always feel a little weird about interacting with those online. She isn't the first lookalike or scary fan I've dealt with, but she may be the most accurate lookalike and now the most eccentric. After whatever this is, she is a certified psychopath in my book. I need to try and find a way out of this forced playdate.

"Thankfully, I got wind of your travel arrangement and knew my daddy had some friends in the Netherlands. I knew they were shady fuckers, but boy oh boy did I underestimate just how shady." She reaches into the open duffle and begins laying out tools that look more surgical than tortuous . . . maybe that's the point. I feel my skin tighten up at the sight of them. The sound they make as she sets them onto the table magnifies the screams I just heard from next door, only now I hear my own wailing through the suffering. Like a premonition of me singing my final song in this concrete studio of my undoing.

"You mean you set this all up?"

"Well, my daddy actually did. He bankrolled the whole thing. You know how old rich men are, they just wanna throw around their dicks, their money, and spoil their princesses."

"You really are batshit crazy!" I'm unable to bite my tongue. I'm terrified and practically helpless but I've never been great about knowing when to keep my mouth shut. "What are you going to do with me then?"

"Me? Batshit crazy?" she says back to me, with a pair of forceps in her hand and surprise plastered across her face. Her jaw hangs open. "I wouldn't say I'm *crazy*, I'm just your number one fan. Some might even say I'm even a bit of . . ." She opens the forceps and smiles at me before closing them again. "A collector."

Collector. That's one way of justifying being insane.

"How about we just have a conversation? Let's just talk. Maybe there's something we can arrange. Please!" Oh great, now I'm begging. Considering how I'm bound and being held prisoner in a foreign country, I don't feel as pathetic as I would otherwise.

Aimee laughs in response. At first it starts small and then becomes a roar. "You can't even respond to a simple message online, what makes you think I would trust you to talk now?" She raises a scalpel to the light, making sure I see it as she twirls it through her fingers like a drummer does their drumsticks. "Besides . . . it just feels a little less than genuine now. But I do have one question though." She sets the tool down beside the others and steps out to strike a pose where I can see her full body. "What do you think of our matching outfits?"

I position myself to stand up, unsure what she's about to do. I don't answer her about the outfit.

"No matter. I think it will make for a great selfie when I'm done."

"Done with what exactly?"

"I'm so glad you asked," she says, going back to her bag of medical supplies. "I have always considered myself your number one fan. And after the first few reconstructive facial surgeries to look just like you, I think I've achieved that. Being the biggest collector of your things was fun, it filled a void in my life for a while, but one day I looked around and it just wasn't enough anymore. I thought of the perfect way for me to be the biggest undisputed no-doubt Phoebe Fox fan in the world. It's one thing to look like someone . . . but it's next level to have their heart."

12

"You want my *heart*?" I ask, baffled at the idea that she would want my beating heart.

She twists her mouth with an eyebrow raised. "Oh, don't be so uptight, Phoebe. I realize that I can't put it up on a shelf or anything, like it's a signed record or something."

"If I'm your favorite person in the world, why would you want to kill me?"

"You may be my favorite person, sure, but I think you've put out enough music that I can enjoy everything that you're touring right now. Your little 'Through the Years' tour seems more like a farewell tour now, huh?"

This bitch is actually a complete psycho. The security team was aware of her as a risk. She always seemed fanatical, but harmless. This is the worst way to find out we were wrong.

"You can't really expect to get away with this!"

"Oh, love, there are precautions in place with The Exhibit when it comes to things like this. I *will* get away with this. And when I'm done here, you and I will be closer than any two people can possibly be."

"What's that supposed to mean?"

Aimee's phone dings and she reaches into one of the side pockets in her duffle bag to retrieve it. "You see," she starts while staring at her screen. "When I'm not on social media or in front of a camera professionally looking like you for money, I've been in school, hell, for the last decade now, to become a heart surgeon. It was something I was pursuing just as I became fond of your music."

Classic example of social media only curating what is wanted to be seen. I can't help but be surprised at that.

"So wait . . . you plan to cut out my fucking heart?"

"Oh, wow! There is already an article floating around that you're missing," Aimee snickers as she thumbs her phone screen intently, ignoring my question while she finishes typing. She's looking at her phone, smiling like she's proud of herself.

An article already? I can't imagine what the world is saying, or how much they know.

Aimee slides her phone back into her duffle bag. "Sorry, ADHD. What was the question?"

"You're planning to cut my heart out?"

Aimee smiles again, like she's fighting back laughter. "There's more to it than that. That would be too simple." She's pulling out more tools and places a box of gloves on the table top. "The perks of being a heart surgeon is that I can confidently perform the procedure myself and ensure that it's done safely."

"How is killing me safe?"

"Phoebe . . . honey, not *you* . . . your heart."

I jerk my leg and my movement is restricted by the chain. The shackle is beginning to feel heavier and I see the scuff marks from the chain on the boots. The boots and my ankle are the least of my concerns right now though. If this bitch plans to do what she says, I would cut off my own foot if it meant a possible escape. "If you're a heart surgeon you already know then that this isn't exactly an ideal operating room."

Aimee walks over to the cement sink that hangs from the wall and begins to wash her hands. "We're not in America anymore. You should know that it doesn't matter. I always get what I want at the end of the day."

I stress with my clenched fists and wrists against the plastic holding them tight. The pain becomes more excruciating as I try desperately to break the zip tie. The bruising will go away if I can just break free. Even if I do though, there is still the matter of getting out of this ankle cuff. "So you're going to just start cutting into me? What is your actual plan to cut my heart out? I'm having a hard time believing my biggest fan is interested in torturing me."

The sink is turned off with a squeaky turn of the sink handle as a hearty laugh fills the room. Aimee is walking toward me. "Phoebe, I'm not some savage who gets off on other people's suffering. What kind of monster would I have to be?" She continues to laugh like there is some inside joke that I'm on the outside of. Her mannerisms and how she speaks is made even more troubling the longer this goes on. "I plan to administer anesthesia to put you down peacefully. You won't feel or remember a thing. I'll even let you pic the last song you ever hear if it helps sooth your concern . . . cross my heart." She laughs. "Well, maybe cross *your* heart if things go well."

"So you want to have my heart? In your body? Like a transplant? Why?"

"To be close to you, obviously."

"How!? You can't perform surgery on yourself."

"That's true . . . luckily, I've already arranged a heart surgeon here in Amsterdam that is willing to do it without all that pesky paperwork. All I need to do is keep your heart on ice and safe and he is on-call when I'm ready. I've thought of everything so that *our* heart can live on without complication."

"You've gone off the deep end, Aimee. Seriously, do you even hear yourself!?" I wrench my hands back and forth even more desperate to snap this plastic and do something. I don't know what that is, but anything is better than just letting this lunatic do whatever she pleases.

Her face hardens and she twists her lips, looking eerily like me, but the expression isn't one I make at all. She stares for a moment. "You know, I only told you all of that because I thought you would be proud of me."

I laugh with a single burst of air. "Proud of you!?"

"Yeah! I thought you'd be pretty impressed with me, actually!"

"Okay, well . . . I'm not. Who kills their favorite person, someone they want to be so bad?"

"You don't get it, Phoebe. It's not about me or you!"

"Think of all of the people you're letting down. This tour ends if I don't get out of here, you know that right?"

Aimee stands there with a flat look. Unreadable as the quiet constricts us. Her lip pulls up with her left cheek as she shakes her head. "I have to apologize, you're not gonna wake up to finish your tour. I am sad about it. I know you don't think so, but for what it's worth . . ."

"Just let me out of here, please. This isn't you. I know you, I've seen you for years." Maybe if I try to really see her I can break through to the actual human being in there.

"To think, Ireland would be your final show, and so many adoring fans had no idea at the time."

Aimee turns her back to me and begins placing her tools on a metal tray not too far from where I'm sitting. I bet if I could get my hands separated that I could possibly reach for them.

"I guess I should be grateful that I got to see you perform in L.A. and Atlanta back in the states. And then I was at the Ireland show because, how could I not, knowing where we'd be right now. Life is so funny sometimes. You know?"

As she's prepping her utensils to essentially murder me, my instinct is telling me that this might be the right time to do what Aaron taught me and break this zip tie. As Aimee is on her soapbox listening to herself talk, I am mentally preparing myself to break out. But I need a plan. What's next once my hands are free?

"Your show last night was amazing by the way. I swear, you just get better and better every time. How do you do it?"

I stand up, staring a hole through Aimee as her back is to me. I can feel the searing rage through the expression on my face while I try not to breathe too loud. With one leg free, I'm able to raise my knee freely to do what I need to do. I might only have one shot at this so I need to give it everything I've got.

"And Phoebe, I don't want you to worry too much about what happens after I'm finished. Your body won't go to waste. Your vital organs I've already made arrangements with buyers and transplant recipients looking for much needed organs on the black market. It's wild what you can find on the dark web if you just look. People are fucking crazy out there."

I raise my hands high above my head. My eyes close and I prepare to try and break the zip tie. Please please please work!

"At the end of the day though, this is an exhibit, I am your artist, which makes you my canvas, and I am so honored to have the privilege to-" I slam my hands down as I raise my knee with all of the force I can muster. I roar like it's my last breath as the plastic snaps against my thigh. The zip tie falls to the ground and everything is in slow motion now. No time for thinking, only action.

Aimee turns around and says something, but I can't hear her words. I only see red as she reaches for a saw that looks more like a power drill. I shove her against the table and she drops the tool. All the other items she carefully placed rattle off the tray and scatter onto the floor. My heartbeat pounds in my ear, almost deafening.

Aimee bends to grab her saw but before she can get a grip on it, I grab a handful of her hair and a wig comes off. She stands there, baffled, with a hand on her head like she's embarrassed. I toss the wig aside and before I can do anything she's lunging at me. She shoves me into the chair and all I can do is fight to keep her hands off of my throat. Her strength and ferocity is terrifying. Up close, face to face, I can see in her expression now all of the subtle differences from her identity to mine. I can see in her eyes that she expected this to go easier. She wasn't expecting a fight.

I manage to twist her arm, using her own strength against her to throw her off balance. With this opening, I explode up from the seat and grab her by the ears and whip her head as hard as I can into the edge of the table near us. She doesn't go down like I hoped and isn't even stunned. Only more feral as she goes low and tackles me. The chain on my ankle catches and causes me to go down. She is on top of me and punches me in the nose and instantly I feel the warmth of blood rushing out. Her hands find my throat and the pressure of her grip spells doom for me. There is no fair fight and I only want to live. I try to pry her hands from my throat as she drives a knee into my midsection. I feel like she might break a rib. No luck in getting her to let up.

I search around the ground, reaching for anything at all that I can get my hand on as my heartbeat bangs louder inside my head.

Cold and unforgiving cement is all I feel.

The leg of the chair that's bolted to the floor is there but offers no help.

That's when I find something hard and skinny. Without realizing what it is I grab it and feel a sharp point. I find the handle and jam the tip into her side as many times as I can—frantically—until she lets me go. I must have stabbed her four times before she let up and stumbled.

My nose continues to spew crimson down my face and chest, ruining this yellow corset. I guess this means we aren't exactly twinning anymore. Not with all this blood.

She holds her side where now she wears her own bloodstains. She reaches again for the power tool and I'm able to kick her. She topples over and the tool knocks loose, bouncing across the room. I go after her again. I can't allow her to get the upper hand again. I stab her shoulder and she slaps me, causing me to stumble back. She pulls the scalpel from her shoulder and tosses it to the floor and is on top of me again. We roll around, grappling and fighting for control—the chain keeping me at a disadvantage.

The chain . . . I think of how I could use this to my benefit as she is on top of me and pinning down one of my legs. I use my free leg, thankful for flexibility, and I get it around her head and now I have her in a head-scissors maneuver. I feel like a cage fighter as I flex my legs and tighten them around her neck. The skirt hiked up, but I don't even care. I only care about squeezing as hard as I've ever squeezed before.

She digs her nails into my calf and my thigh, but the adrenaline makes me feel invincible. I squeeze and squeeze. Her body kicks and flails like a fish out of water and I raise my hips off the floor to put even more pressure on her. In the movies, it doesn't take long for someone to die or give up the fight, but this lasts a lot longer than that. I twist my hips to add more torque and to get a tighter grip around her throat with my legs. Her eyes bulge as her complexion transforms into a shade unfamiliar. I can feel her death throes as we both fight for our lives. Only one of us was meant to leave this room.

the **HG** Report

Hot People. Hot Gossip. No Bullshit.

PHOEBE FOX DITCHES AMSTERDAM

By Kayla Riceburough | August 3rd, 2025 | 6:52 a.m.

An inside source from Phoebe Fox's team has confirmed that she and her security entourage never checked into the private villa where she would be staying for the Netherlands leg of the 'Through The Years' Tour. With Fox grinding on the biggest international tour (in history) some people on her team are speculating that the allure of the Red Light District may be a contributing factor in her detour.

After photos recently surfaced of Phoebe being a little too close to another musician, it's not much of a stretch to think she is shacking up with a new squeeze in Europe.

After another weekend of sold out stadium dates, Phoebe [Fox] left Ireland and arrived in the Netherlands with a full agenda leading up to the series of shows being put on in Amsterdam.

For more scandalous reports on Phoebe Fox, you can follow **POP CULTURE PLANET** for more news on all things Phoebe Fox!

If you are dying to know what celebrities we think Phoebe Fox would be perfect to date, **CLICK HERE**
Follow Trending #whereisphoebefox

poplover03: Where the hell is Phoebe???

@irish_girllyy: I hope everything is alright 🫶

@phoebe_memes: She better not fucking cancel! I paid too much for these tickets and already booked a flight and hotel!

@my.life.is.a.concert: This is FAKE NEWS!!! She always comes through! The gig isn't even for another FIVE days! Y'all need to chill tf out. **#PhoebeFoxTour**

@moooon.chick04: I mean, maybe she just stayed somewhere else. Why is this even news?

@redsox4lyfe: Probably hiding somewhere writing shitty music about her new BF **#PhoebeFoxSucks**

@ItsJustAimee13: Hearing that Phoebe possibly won't make her next show absolutely cuts my heart out! 😣

@musclesnbeer: So who is she dating now?

@phoebefoxmemes2023: If I were in Amsterdam with that much money I'd skip the tour and hit the Red Light District too! 😅

13

Aimee's struggle ceases as I notice her fingernails stop digging into my thigh. I rock my hips from side to side a few more times to ensure she's done. With no next step in this last ditch effort, I look around the room at the mess of surgical tools splayed along the floor. The chain is still secure and holding me prisoner with my number one fan's motionless body still being held in the lethal deathgrip of my legs. I'm afraid to release her because I don't know if she is dead or just unconscious.

I loosen the grip and ease her head onto the floor, thankful that she isn't moving or surprising me with a final burst of energy like in those cheesy scary movies. I place two fingers on her neck and feel for any sign of life . . . Nothing, she isn't breathing, so I take a deep breath in relief.

"Shit, shit, shit," I mutter as I search her body in hopes for a key or something. I couldn't get that lucky, especially with her dressed exactly like me. "Fuck."

I hear my heartbeat in my ears as I try to keep myself from panicking and as the beating pulse calms in my head I hear the man screaming once more from the other side of the wall behind me. I can't help but think that could have been me screaming alongside him right now. The terrifying sound of a powertool screeching in tune with his screams only heightens my need to get the hell out of this room and fast. I get to my feet and look around for something within my reach I can use to defend myself with. The bloody scalpel that Aimee tossed aside after being stabbed with it catches my eye. It's just a small sharp blade but might as well be a loaded gun compared to having nothing at all.

I cringe at the sounds I hear from the other room. My nose is still bleeding as I wipe my face with the back of my hand, wincing at the touch. I'm pretty sure my nose is broken. Bright red and fresh blood stains my hand and as I stand here processing what to do I hear the whining from the hinges as the door opens.

"No . . . shit," I say, unsure what to do now. I drop the scalpel on the floor and stand on it in hopes to not be seen with a weapon. One of the men who had been my chaperone, the less talkative one, comes into the room and looks at me and then the body near my feet.

"What's this?" the man asks, nodding to the body on the floor.

I don't have a plan . . . but I also don't freeze.

I improvise.

My expression changes to one of confidence as I rattle the chain with a shake of my leg. "I'll tell you what all of this is, this bitch, Phoebe Fox somehow got loose and got ahold of me!" I pause for his reaction and he only looks confused. I'm stunned that this might actually work. This may be the only time ever that I'm grateful for Aimee being such a good impersonator, and thank God we're also dressed the same. "Don't just stand there, you imbecile! Unlock this damn chain this instant!"

My own tone feels so entitled and unlike me as the words tumble out of my mouth. I can't help but wonder if I would have made a good actress. He makes slow strides over with his gaze moving from Aimee and to me. Both of us, covered in blood and all of the evidence of an altercation. I can see him playing detective and not really putting it together. "How she get out?"

"Uh, duh, whoever put her in here *obviously* didn't make sure it was locked," I respond, in the bitchiest way I can muster.

"I lock myself, I have key right here," he says, pulling the single little silver key from his shirt pocket.

"Okay, well how else would I end up with my ankle in this shackle? Stop stalling and let me out already. You wouldn't want me to tell my father, would you?"

He stares at me, stone-faced while he chews on the inside of his cheek. I can't tell if he is onto my terrible plan or not but I hold an impatient wide-eyed stare at him. The kind that says, *Hurry the fuck up, stupid.* The moment lasts only a few seconds but feels like an eternity before he makes his way toward me and crouches down. "You American girls. Always so stupid. Such brats." He unlocks the shackle.

"Just get me out of this. Would have been nice if you had come sooner!" I say as he pulls it from my boot and I can't believe it. I'm free! Now what? I have this guard to contend with and he thinks I'm Aimee.

I squat down as he is standing up and I grab the scalpel from under my boot. His walkie talkie scrambles with staticky air. "Anton, what's your location?" a voice asks. As he reaches for the walkie and turns his head, I stand up and with the handle trapped in my tight fist and I jam the blade up, feeling it slide into the underside of his jaw. I release a primal scream as his hand shoots up to grab his chin but I continue to stab, yelling with each swing. Each stab goes into the top of his hand and under his jaw. He tries to grab me with his other hand and I continue stabbing. I hit his neck and can see the desperation in his eyes. It's a weird thing to read in someone's eyes. To see the fear and regret in someone's face, absent of words, but perfectly communicated that they know they fucked up. The blood doesn't just run out. It spurts like a water balloon with a pin hole.

He clutches his neck with one hand and reaches for his gun with the other and I pounce on him, pushing him into the wall, causing him to stumble and fall. The gun shakes free and hits the floor and I seize the moment. I'm on top of him and I stab the exposed part of his throat that his hand isn't protecting. So much blood rushes out of the new holes in his body. Not the look of a tough guy, not the look of a militant goon, but the look of a scared boy in a man's body.

I stop my flurry of stabs and he stops trying to stop me. His eyes stay locked onto me as I watch his eyes become vacant and his hands fall away. His stare becomes empty and he bleeds out just within arm's reach of Aimee's body and now I'm free to leave this room. The blood stains my clothes while the calm lifeless faces haunt my mind. I can't worry about that right now. I need to get out of here and find help.

The walkie talkie on the man's belt sounds with white noise. "Anton, do you copy? Over."

"I repeat . . . Do you have copy? Over."

Only a second to screw my head on straight after everything that's just happened and now I have to figure out what to do next. People are going to come looking for this big man named Anton and I don't sound like a man.

"Anton, respond!"

I squat down and grab the gun from his holster that he was reaching for, ready to blow anyone's head off who tries to stop me. There's just one problem though . . . I have no clue how to use it.

I need to get out of here before whoever is on the other end of that radio comes looking. I study the handgun with the same look that I might stare at an alien spaceship in the sky. The little button that toggles on the side that shows red must be the safety. I flip it back to not show. I hope like hell I don't have to point this at anyone, but I will if I have to . . . I just hope it fires when I do. I stand by the heavy door and listen outside as I work up the courage to leave this room. My eyes keep pulling to the two people lying dead on the floor.

Dead by *my hands*.

My stomach wants to sink as my chest tightens, but everything else in my body and brain are screaming for me to run out of here and never look back. I don't even know where I am though, and if I make it out of here I have to have a place to go. Some place that can call for help.

"Alright, time to be brave, Phoebe," I whisper.

I turn the handle and the door is heavier than it looks as the hinges protest motion. I cringe at the sound of metal on metal scraping and singing a song that carries through the hallway. I only open just enough to walk out. I pop my head out and look in both directions. To my left, a long stretch of concrete walls and doors spaced apart on both sides. To my right, not as far down, but more of the same with the spaced out doors. Metal shelving units line the walls near the end and heavy metal music can be heard faintly from somewhere in that direction.

The smell of warm dust and hot wires invade my nose and I realize how ridiculous I look dressed like this. On stage I'm a megastar, but here, I feel like a stripper. I take off the long white boots and leave them behind. The heel doesn't seem practical for running and if I need to take off in a hurry I can't be worrying about proper footwear.

Alright, here we go. My gut says to go right, so I shuffle down the hall with the gun held tight against my palm. The floor is cold against the bottoms of my feet and I can feel the filth sticking to them with each step. I stop at the first door and curiosity makes me pause for a moment. I hear the powertool and the man screaming on the other side of the door. A reminder of being trapped as I waited for my death only moments ago. I can't let whoever is in there continue to suffer. I have this gun, maybe I can save someone else too. I don't think I could live with myself knowing I could have tried and didn't. My finger massages the trigger while I stare at the gun and feel braver having it.

I slowly ease my eyes to the dirty window in the door and I can see a man in a long coat wearing a strange mask with some kind of power saw. The other man is in a chair—not much different from the one I was in—strapped to it. The masked man raises the tool and as I hear it come to life I imagine him doing unspeakable things to this man with me watching as an unintended audience. I can't watch, I *have* to do something!

Without hesitation, I turn the handle and I force the door open as quickly as I can and stumble in with the gun raised and aimed right at the man in the mask. I get a better look at it and it's just a clear mask that makes his face underneath blurry and impossible to identify. I can see dark eyes though. Eyes that look surprised to see me. He stares back at me and lowers the saw and holds up his other hand.

The guy being tortured doesn't look up. His head hangs and he only weeps. There is so much blood on the floor around him and it covers the front of the man in the mask as well. It looks like a can of red paint exploded. His coat—looking like something a doctor would wear—is covered in blood.

"Drop it!" I say, summoning all of the confidence I can as my finger hugs the trigger.

"Just relax, ma'am," he says as he takes a step toward me.

"I said drop it! Stop where you are!" I raise the gun to his head and point it at him more aggressively.

He stops, raising the power saw again. I can't see his face but I can see his eyes. He is looking me up and down, sizing me up.

"Help . . ." the man in the chair chokes out. I look over for only a second to see him raising his head, and in that fraction of a moment the man in the mask lunges at me. The saw screams with its whirring grind and without a second thought, I squeeze the trigger.

POP!

The sound reverberates off the thick concrete walls surrounding us. It's so much louder than I expected.

"Agh!" he wails as the saw drops and he clutches his collarbone, staggering back.

My heart slams against my chest. The same heart that was almost taken from me in this godforsaken place. Understanding that only makes me wonder what this psychopath's plan was for this poor guy.

"You fucking bitch!" he shouts in an accent I can't quite place. His face is blurry with the mask on but I can see evil in his eyes as he ignores the gun that just shot him. He makes fast steps in my direction.

"Back up, motherfucker!" When my words aren't taken as a warning, I tense up with the gun raised and squeeze again.

POP! POP!

My ears ring and I can't help but bring my hands to my ears. The masked man falls back and hits the floor like a bag of sand. I lean forward to look at him as I point the gun awkwardly and see the clear mask filling with blood and even more spreading out onto the floor.

Paralyzed at the ringing that echoes from the gunfire, I freeze.

I've killed three people in a matter of minutes and all were threatening my life. I know I don't deserve this, and maybe they didn't either . . . but what was I to do? His body doesn't move and neither do I—only my quivering lip as I feel lost, staring at the red pool that saturates the floor around his head.

"Help . . ." the man in the chair rattles off a nasty cough. "Me."

I snap out of it. "Yes, sorry. Let's get you out of here."

I think about hearing his agonizing screams seeping through the wall behind me. I imagine us back to back with the bricks separating us while his screams give me a snippet of what might be me next. I wonder if he knows I heard his most vulnerable moments while I race to unfasten the leather straps keeping his arms restrained, and then the same to his feet, and the one around his chest. There is so much blood on him. Still wet to the touch as I free him from the straps. He raises his head, struggling to hold himself up to look at me. I catch his eyes, but as I see the rest of his face my hand shoots over my mouth to keep from screaming.

Blood drips in long strings that pour from his lips like strawberry syrup. The bottom part of his face, under his nose, his chin, and up to his ears has been removed leaving only exposed muscle and tendons with so much congealed blood.

He tries to stand and his legs shake, struggling to hold up his weight as he collapses back into the chair.

"Come on, I got you," I say as I swoop in and throw his arm around my neck and try to help him up as best as I can.

"I'm only gonna slow you down . . ." I feel his legs giving out as he tries to stand by himself.

"No, we have to get you out of here. I can't leave you behind after what–" I muscle him up to try and get some semblance of a pace as we stagger to the door. I'm practically dragging him but he starts to use his legs. "Someone had to have heard the gunshots. We need to move, quick." We get into the hallway and head toward the racks along the wall.

"You have to leave me, I'm no . . . good," he says through a pained cough.

We continue trudging along, dragging ourselves across the dirty floor. "We're going to get somewhere safe. We're gonna get you to a hospital, and–"

"Freeze!"

"Stop!"

Two voices call out from behind us and we hear shuffling boots coming toward us from the other end of the hallway. I don't want to stop. I want to move forward and get out of here. Even though I'm committed to saving . . . I don't even know his name. Despite my best intentions, he's going to just slow me down and I fear that at some point I may have to leave him behind. I feel awful even thinking that, but the reality is just that.

"Halt! Or we shoot!"

Fuck.

15

I stop at the mention of them shooting. I hear hurried footsteps behind us that echo in the hallway. I look at my new travel companion and he's not doing well.

"We're not gonna . . . make it out alive," he says with every bit of pain and defeat carrying his words. "Just go on without me. You can still move. You can still run. I'm already dead."

"Don't talk like that," I say to him, trying to sound reassuring, but I know in my heart that he's probably right.

"Don't move!" one of the men shouts as they approach.

The injured man on my arm reaches up and feels his face and immediately starts to cry out against his own touch. I can't stop myself from cringing at his reaction as the shivers move through me. His face oozes blood that glazes over dried blood where so much facial muscle is exposed. It looks really bad, it has to feel even worse. Fuzzy memories of washing and sanitizing in a restroom when I had a cut on my hand come to mind. I imagine that stinging on my face, only with the pain turned way up.

His cries quickly become weeping. "You have to keep it together. We're gonna get out of here and get you help."

He shakes his head *no* letting out broken breathing patterns between his sobbing. "Just kill me."

"What, no!"

"Please."

"Put your hands . . . above your head," the man commands, slow and enunciating clearly.

I hesitate. Knowing I have a gun means I don't have to surrender just because they tell me to. "Just play along," I say to the man beside me.

I turn around quickly and point the gun and the approaching men stop. Both men point their guns at us and look surprised to see me brandishing a weapon. "Drop the gun, Miss Fox!" one of the men orders.

"Why in the fuck would I do that!?" I scream. "So you can just shoot me anyway? I don't think so."

"We no want to shoot you, but we will."

I feel the weight on my shoulder relieved as the injured man stumbles forward, staggering toward the men with his shambling legs. "You want to shoot someone? Shoot me, you sacks of shit!"

"No! What are you doing!?" I ask, not even knowing his name, watching him lumber ahead, provoking the patrolmen with his insults.

"Freeze, stay!"

"What if I don't?" he asks, still dragging himself in their direction. "You don't have the balls to shoot me, look at you, with your–"

Bang!

Bang! Bang!

Bang!

The man takes every bullet and falls sideways into the wall before crashing to the floor.

"Miss Fox, you drop gun. Now!"

I can't bring myself to do it, but I'm walking backwards, ready to turn and run at any moment.

"That z'enough!" a man shouts, seemingly appearing from out of nowhere. He walks between the two men with guns, dressed in military garb, with what sounds like a French accent, carrying his English words when he speaks.

I stand completely awestruck about witnessing them shooting that man. My eyes pull to his limp body but panic pulls them back to the gunmen. I feel my heart trying to escape from my chest.

The well-dressed French man paces, sizing up the two gunmen. "You two cannot damage z'goods. She does not belong to us. We must take her alive, unharmed." He turns to me. "Come along now, Phoebe. Don't z'make zis any harder than it needs to be."

"I'm not coming with you. Not without a fight. You're gonna have to kill me here."

The man smirks. "Phoebe Fox, z'most iconic person in pop culture. It vould be easy to kill you here and do vhat we would with your corpse... You vould be taken to a room, cleaned up and picked to pieces and sold to z'folks needing a kidney, a lung, maybe skin, eyes, and then to people with more of an... acquired taste for exotic delicacies, if you know what I mean. People around z'world vould wonder where you went, others vould speculate, but no one vould know what really happened to you." He stares at the dead man on the floor and quickly turns to face me directly. "But you do not belong to us. Someone paid a lot of money for you."

He snaps his finger.

"Take her alive," he says to the men. "Come along now, Miss Fox, that z'nough trouble out of you."

The two men with their guns aimed at me begin to take steps toward me as I continue to take faster paced steps back. "I belong to no one," I say with the gun raised as I aim at the French man and pull the trigger.

Click.

Shit, it's empty!

"Seize her!" he orders, roaring as his demeanor becomes more agitated. "No guns!"

I pull the trigger again, feeling the resistance of the trigger without the satisfaction of loud noise to follow. As the men lower their weapons I throw the handgun at one of them and take off running away.

It's all instinct.

There is no plan.

I don't know where I'm at, other than it's a filthy shithole. I have no sense of a way out, all of the doors look the same.

"Everyone. Z'girl is on the run. Take her alive," I hear the French man say over radio static.

I barrel down the hall, bare feet smacking against the smooth concrete as two men give chase. I take comfort knowing they've been ordered not to shoot me, but it would be nice to know how many of them are here. I pull down one of the big shelving units along the wall and the men stutter their feet to a stop as the metal frame and shelves come crashing down with everything else. I consider how exhausted and weak I feel despite this, but the adrenaline in me clearly has taken over. The clashing of metal and random items make plenty of noise, and leave a bigger mess as I pull down another rack beside it and it falls fast and just as loud. The end closest to the first rack knocks against it and stands tilted, creating a convenient obstruction as the men try to climb over—allowing me to put space between them and I.

I come to the end where I can turn left or right. I take a left, not wasting any time to overthink. I stop at the first door and jiggle the handle and it's locked. I rush down further to another door and it's also not opening.

Panic is setting in as desperation takes a foothold. I go to a third door on the end of the hall where the door opens with no issue. I fall in and close the door quickly without letting it slam. I look around and I'm not sure what this room is, but I can tell right away that there is no other way out. This door at my back is the one and only way out, and I can't help but to feel like I just waltzed right into my own tomb.

@antoniodances: We haven't heard from Phoebe, but this article is just clickbait. If you really know her then you KNOW this is just desperate reporting. So sad that people believe anything they read on the internet.

@its.me.darlene.baby: This doesn't seem like her to just ghost everyone. Something must be really wrong. 😢

@user7666137776h4uzz00: Have the police been notified?

@randysaid: This is why I spend my money on more practical things. No sense making this rich bitch even richer. 🙄

@suspishus.behaviour: Soooo the show is or isn't happening?

@aaron_ashley.winters: Thoughts and Prayers for her and her team

@cast.a.spell_12: I know I didn't just spend $5000 on travel and tickets to surprise my fiance for her to just not show up. What. The. F#$% 😡

@allie_kat_here: Has anyone heard from her mom???

16

My chest rises and falls as the wind comes out in bursts. My eyes crawl about the room, taking in the space.

What *is* this room?

Two stainless steel tables sit in the center of the room, side by side but with enough space between them to move around. I see carts of surgical utensils and other tools that don't look so sterile. An alarm clock radio puts harmonics into the space, but nothing I can recognize. More shelving cabinets line three of the walls. I hustle over to the cabinets and there's a folding table with clothes and other random items. The clothes that I was wearing when I was taken—along with the bracelet—lay on the table in a small pile beside other clothes and personal items I don't recognize. I can't help but wonder if any of this belonged to the nameless man I tried to help who's now dead in the hallway.

STRONG ENOUGH.

I take the bracelet and slip it on as I hustle over to inspect the cabinets along the wall. I pull back a heavy sheet and notice they aren't cabinets at all, but shelves built into the wall with large metal trays like you might see in a bakery—or in a mortuary.

Holy shit! Is this where they bring the people when they're done? Aimee mentioned that no one goes to waste. And that French guy too!

I climb onto one of the lower trays and hide myself. A thick curtain hangs where I can stay out of sight, but also can't see anything.

I close my eyes and try to calm myself—at least as much as one can try to in this situation. I'm committed to getting out of here, but can't escape that voice in the back of my head telling me that I'm completely screwed. The tray is cold against my skin as I adjust my body, desperate to not make more noise than needed. As I lay still waiting, the music continues. Voices in another language that sound beautiful through the imperfect scratchy signal play an upbeat rhythm that my heartbeat is not matching as I try not to breathe any louder than the music.

The door flies open, banging against the wall as thunderous feet rush into the room.

"Where's girl?" a familiar voice says.

"I no see her."

The men who chased me. They didn't take long to climb over my obstacle course.

"Do you think she's in locked rooms?"

"Maybe," he says. Loud metal rattles as a cart bangs. "She can't escape. They'll have our heads. We search room! She might be hiding."

"Like filthy rat!"

More rifling through things ensues. I flinch with each offensive crash as these men are not gentle with their search. They start to go back and forth in another language and I can't follow what they're saying. My cheeks tense up and I lay quietly with my eyes tightly shut, wishing them to go away.

"Fuck!" one of them exclaims. My eyes wander, inspecting for a crack, or a sliver of light so maybe I can see out. As I tilt my head back to see better I can see the tray on the shelf beside me and what I see elicits a yelp that I'm quick to trap with a hand covering my mouth. A foot is visible mere inches from my face, and as my eyes stare at it longer, I notice the blood where it's been severed. Fingers and hunks of flesh occupy the tray and suddenly the smell is potent. I can't tell if it's the tears or the smell that sting my eyes as I fight to not make a peep.

I hear the thick curtains being flung open. No, no, no! They're checking. They're gonna find me. I need a plan. I can fight, but I don't stand a chance against two of these men.

Another curtain, much closer, is flung open, threatening that I'll be found next when the door opens and the frantic search is brought to a stop.

"Hey! What the hell are you two doing in my office!?" a man with an arrogant tone in his voice asks. Perfect English.

"Phoebe Fox, she's gotten away from us. We think she might be in–"

"I don't give a damn if she sucks your mother's dick while you suck your daddy's," he interrupts with that odd visual. "You don't get to come into my space and start tearing up my things? Who's gonna clean this up? Are you?"

Whoever that is, he is clearly entitled by the pitch of his whiny, yet confident voice.

"She belongs to Wayne Silverman, we must find–"

"Fuh-fuh-fuck off! Get the fuck out of here! If she was here, don't you think you'd see her?"

"We need to make sure."

"I said get the fuck out of here before I have you reprimanded! I've got work to do!"

Silence lingers for a moment and I can imagine an intense stare-down happening on the other side of the thick curtain that suddenly feels razor thin, considering that it's all that hides me away from prying eyes.

"Go on, shoo!"

"If you see anything, you call us."

"Fine, whatever, go!"

The American voice follows the footsteps and the door closes.

"Jesus-fucking-Christ. I'm gone, not even ten minutes."

The American that runs this . . . *office* . . . paces around. It sounds like he's cleaning up while making snide comments to himself. I hear his grunts as he squats down to pick things up.

I need a plan. I feel stuck, and somehow in an even worse situation than before. Only now, everyone is looking for me. Somehow, this guy doesn't seem to care though.

I lay quiet as a mouse, pretending the smell isn't the most putrid thing I've ever inhaled. I find myself getting lost in thoughts as I wait for an opening. An opening for what, I don't know yet. I don't know what time it is but I can't help but to think about my fans. The tens of thousands that are probably confused and upset that I'm not at the stadium. The pang of guilt hits me thinking about the people who shelled out so much money, and then traveled from afar just to see me perform. I can only imagine what sort of rumors are spreading about me.

My security team . . . my friends. All dead. Does anyone know? Are police investigating? Am I even considered missing yet, technically?

I think about Ashton, and our last interaction. My heart skips a beat and I can feel it in my throat at the thought of him learning that I've gone missing. He's had to have called me several times by now. He must be worried sick, and here I am feeling guilty. Was the dressing room in Ireland our last kiss?

The American walks over and stops right in front of me. His big body casts a shadow, even through the dark curtain. I can feel his presence, his heavy breathing amplified more by his closeness. The curtain flings open, but he still doesn't know I'm here.

This is it. I'm totally exposed now.

He is doing something on the shelf above me. I can hear him moving things around. His body odor somehow manages to break through the already rancid smell that I'm simmering in. His gut hangs out of his shirt as he reaches up. His hairy belly taunts me as I imagine him finding me and how difficult it might be to get away from him if he gets his hands on me.

I can't allow that to happen.

I need to get ahead of this.

He begins humming along to the song on the radio, dancing as his belly sways too close to my face. He wears baggy pants with a drawstring and I can see the outline of his bulge as he moves. The radio goes to a commercial and I don't know what they're saying at all, but the American with the belly—and bulge now in my face—begins to sing one of *my* songs. It's hard to not be disgusted. It's almost like the universe is taunting me now while this gluttonous man dances and sings one of my more popular and upbeat songs.

His voice is atrocious to anyone's ears and as the chorus hits his voice goes up several octaves that only show how much he shouldn't be singing. He seems to be having a good time though, singing in a whiny and feminine voice.

Is that what he thinks I sound like?

I need to do something . . . quick, before he finds out I've been here this whole time.

What are the benefits of waiting? If he steps away and doesn't close the curtain, he'll definitely see me. I'm not sure playing dead will matter.

If I make a move now, I risk a fight that I'm not ready to have. Also, what if the others come back? If he screams, will they hear?

Am I overthinking this?

I need to be smart, but I need to survive.

My eyes keep following his overhanging gut as he shuffles side to side. His awful singing continues and if I'm going to make a move, I need to make it happen right now.

My eyes close tight as I take in a gulp of tainted air. I feel the stinging tears at the corners of my eyes, and even more as I open them again just a moment later. Something takes over me and I lose all control. Maybe flight mode. Maybe a will to live. I reach out, grabbing ahold of his genitals, really digging in with the tightest grip I possibly can.

He staggers back, his singing becoming a surprised, albeit higher pitch squeal. "Whatthefuck, whatthefuck!?" My hold only hardens as he steps back once more, enough to pull me out of hiding, making me a secret no more. I look up, trying to get to my feet, unwilling to loosen my grip at all. "Get the fuck off me you fucking cunt!"

I feel his hand take a handful of my hair as he jerks my head back with so much force I yelp like a dog having its tail stepped on.

"Get off of me!" he demands, but more like begging just before I'm tugged the other way more aggressively.

My teeth clench and I feel the hairs popping off my scalp against his urgent pulling. It hurts like hell . . . but I've got him by the balls and only squeeze harder in response.

I try to stand, my feet shuffling to find their place. That's when he lets my hair go. I feel dizzy, and at the same time relieved, but only for a second before my sight turns bright white against the sudden impact of his fist.

My grip releases and I plummet to the floor, stunned.

The music fades away as a piercing ringing sound cuts through my head. I open my eyes and see the American holding his crotch, hunched over. I stagger from my knees, like a baby deer trying to stand for the first time. After this, I am reborn.

The man comes over with malice, shoving me back onto the floor. I bang into a stretcher and it knocks over. "What the fuck are you doing in here?" he questions, his voice raised as he stands over me, a hulking figure. A shadowy silhouette that blocks out the light at his back.

I don't answer him. I'm still processing being hit. Adrenaline floods my body and I'm sure the pain will catch up later, if there is a later.

He grabs my hair again and flings me across the floor where I fall, offering no resistance this time. "How did you get in here?"

He rolls me onto my back and pins me down. His big, meaty frame is much too enormous of an obstacle to overcome as he leans his body weight—and forearm—into my chest.

I can't breathe.

"You fucking bitch. You tell me right now, you fucking bitch," he wheezes.

I can't find the words to respond. I shove my left hand into his face as I try to find a finger for his eye. He moves his head, careful to avoid. My hand in his face is enough to push him away though.

My right hand reaches around and finds a metal cart, my wandering hand searching for the first thing it can grab onto that can be used as a weapon.

"Fucking answer me!" he screams in my face, spraying me with his spit as he leans in harder. I can feel my breathing becoming more and more difficult. He might crush my chest.

As he leans into me his head is pressed harder against my hand trying to ward him off. My other hand is still flailing around the cart when my fingers dance around what feels like the handle of a pair of scissors—maybe—as I get a grip.

The weight of it, the balance of it, nothing like scissors at all. My fingers curl and pull it into my palm with a vicious clasp as I bring it to his exposed neck quickly in one fluid motion, tearing through his throat. The satisfaction of feeling his weight shift off my chest is intoxicating. I breathe deep and watch him on top of me, his hands clinging to his throat like he's trying to hold his head on. His eyes open wide, like a mask of utter horror—the surprise of what he anticipated to be my imminent death becoming his instead.

The blood seeps through his fingers and in no time at all it's spilling onto me. I look at my hand and see that I'm holding a bonesaw. The tiny serrated teeth glisten with his blood and I look back at him as he tries to stand. More blood gushes from the wound like an arterial faucet of his demise.

I just lay here, watching.

He tries to speak and that only makes matters worse . . . for him at least. Blood breaches his lips, spilling down his chin. He coughs, clearly choking on it. The pressure spurts out as his hand loosens and it sprays onto me, ruining my yellow top even more. This is the most horrific thing I've ever seen in my life, watching this man fighting a losing battle to save himself. I know it, he knows it, and all I can do is watch, thankful that it isn't me bleeding out at an alarming rate.

The blood is thick against my skin and tickles as it drips off me. I scoot away from him as he falls back. He leans against the wall with one hand still trying to keep his blood in his body while staring at me. He doesn't need to speak for me to see he's scared, his eyes give it away. His head rocks into one of his shoulders and his hand drops to his side. The rush of blood that erupts from the slash in his throat is so dark. He doesn't struggle as it saturates his entire front side and pools onto the floor around him, spreading out quickly.

I hold the bonesaw out at him as I rise to my feet.

He stops moving and I watch as the lights go out in his eyes. I stare at my corset and skirt and it's taken on a tie-dyed look of yellow and red with orange hues from all of the blood. I can't help but to laugh. What are the odds? I should have never made it out of the ankle cuff, and died in that room, but instead I've left four bodies in my path to survival and I'm covered in an unbelievable amount of blood like I'm in a horror movie.

Okay, Phoebe, what now?

The Rise of Phoebe Fox - Part 3

With the bright neon lights of the Nashville strip behind her, she had set out to record her first record. Phoebe and her mother would find a recording studio and worked with an engineer who would help produce a handful of her early songs. This was a bit of a learning experience for Phoebe, but once she got a taste for making music, she couldn't stop writing more and more.

Phoebe Fox

I just felt like . . . . I knew in my heart that it was time. I had spent so many nights in my bed just writing poems and lyrics to songs in my head. I had already been playing a lot of those songs on the acoustic guitar for a few years so it made sense that I would see how they could sound as a complete song.

Interviewer

Do you know how many songs you may have written up to that point?

Phoebe Fox

[Blows out a long breath with her eyes wide] I have no idea. I had so many notebooks and journals. Loose scrap paper with words scribbled on them that I stuffed into books.

Interviewer
Just if you had to guess . . .

Phoebe Fox
I'd imagine it had to have been at least a thousand.

Interviewer
Complete songs?

Phoebe Fox
Mmhmm.

Interviewer
That's pretty impressive . . . What can you tell
me about the process of songwriting? I imagine you
have so much that you know you will never get to
record them all.

Phoebe Fox
Well, you're right. I'll never record all of those
songs, but there are times I go through some of
them and I start picking out things I liked from
years ago. Sometimes I start with a recycled lyric,
and I'm able to create a whole new song.

[Home video plays of Phoebe curled up on the couch
with a colorful notepad as she writes, focused on
the page.]

Martha Fox
She had talked a bit about a record deal and
trying to send out some demos after talking to the
producer. It was a really exciting time to be in her
orbit. Things were happening fast. I think by then
everyone could feel that she was onto something
bigger. She was in the studio all day whenever she
could be. After she graduated high school there was
no keeping her out of there.

[A young woman with long dark hair walks onto a new
set. The spotlight turns on and she is on a barstool
in the middle of a stage. She smiles before the name
is displayed on the screen. Naomi Wilde, Recording
Artist.]

[A video montage shows footage of Phoebe in the
studio with Naomi. The visual transitions to Naomi
Wilde and her on stage before a performance,
laughing.]

Naomi Wilde
I met Phoebe at the Soundscape studio, outside of
Nashville. We would always see each other coming or
going. I was in a group at the time and she was so
nice. We just hit it off immediately.

Interviewer
Do you remember the first time you heard her sing?

Naomi Wilde
Oh yeah. I sat in on more than a couple sessions.
We had the same producer and there were nights
where it was just like a big hangout. There were
nights you couldn't make us leave.

Phoebe Fox
Getting to be in the studio with Naomi may be one
of the most special moments for me personally.

Interviewer
What about that point in your career made that
so special?

Phoebe Fox
[Pauses, clearly contemplating her response.]
I think . . . She was sort of at the same cross-
roads as I was. Being around a peer and creative
with a little guidance from professionals, you
know, the engineer, being there for the mix, even
if I wasn't recording I was just as stoked to
be in that environment when she was doing her
record.

[A pixelated vertical video of Phoebe and Naomi
laughing as they take selfie video plays.]

Phoebe Fox
Being around another woman with the same dream, it's
like . . . There is an understanding of the pursuit,
and all we wanted to do was support each other and

other and see how far this dream could go. We
became really tight and I just love her so much.

[A video package shows clips of Phoebe in the
recording booth singing, alternating to Naomi Wilde
in the studio as well. Both are smiling and happy.]

Interviewer
What would you say is the one thing about you that
separates you from other artists in the industry?

*Phoebe would spend the better part of six months
recording a collection of songs with a demo in
mind, but ultimately enough for an album should
she decide to put out her own music. She knew
early enough that if she wanted to be an artist
that it wouldn't be easy. It would take many hours
of hard work, but if she wanted to be a star, it
would require one key ingredient that transcended
passion and talent.*

Phoebe Fox
Obsession.

Hanna Chance
After high school Phoebe spent a lot of time at the
studio and I was starting college. I was trying to
take dance seriously, but at that time I guess we
just naturally drifted a little.

[Video plays of Phoebe sitting at a large studio mixing console with headphones beside the sound engineer.]

Hanna Chance

We still would talk but a lot of times when I would call she would answer but have to go to work on something. She used to invite me but I just didn't know that world and had my own things going on.

Martha Fox

Phoebe had a pile of songs, something for everyone it seemed like. It was so surreal hearing her recorded professionally for the first time. Mixed and mastered. It sounded just as good as the CDs you could buy anywhere. She sounded better!

Naomi Wilde

She was doing something no one else was doing in the music industry at the time. She was writing music for herself, telling her story. She was being authentic. Her songs didn't feel like the standard cookie-cutter format. Her music felt lived in already.

With a batch of finished songs and no clear path it was time to make one. Phoebe and Soundscape producer Shawn Richardson started sending off demos and press kits with headshots to any record label or publisher with an address they could find.

Hanna Chance
Oh my God! Phoebe is flying to New York! She is
getting busy, things are getting serious.

Naomi Wilde
Phoebe and Shawn flew to New York to meet with
someone at Kingdom Records and she came home with
her first record deal two days later.

[Phoebe Fox hugs Shawn Richardson and she shows her
signature on the contract to the camera, jumping up
and down with the most joyous energy.]

Naomi Wilde
I was so happy! I mean, I knew in my gut that she
was going to go places, but it was just so surreal
to see her really do it. She really made a plan
and went out and did it. It made the dream feel
possible for me at the time, before I got signed.

*With the ink still wet, Phoebe went right back into
the studio more motivated than ever. With a fresh
outlook on the world that would await. She set the
tone for a work ethic that would become the stuff of
legend when people talk about her extensive catalog
of music.*

[A video plays of Phoebe singing vocals in the
studio recording booth with large can headphones
on.]

Her debut album would come out when she was only twenty years old .⌧ ⌧ ⌧ ⌧ ⌧ And.it would set the world on fire.

[Video plays of Phoebe playing with a ball of fire, from one of her music videos.]

Martha Fox
Phoebe's album, we all couldn't believe it.
Everything happened so fast.

Naomi Wilde
Her first music video showed up on MTV and VH1 and just caught fire. Radio stations ate it up and before you knew it, everyone wanted a piece of Phoebe.

Hanna Chance
Phoebe's first music video was actually my first professional gig as a dancer! I feel like we both won together with that. I was so happy when she invited me . . . well, insisted that I be in the video.

[Video plays of Hanna and Phoebe rehearsing dance moves with other dancers.]

Hanna Chance
It was a full circle moment for us both.

Martha Fox
Her song *A Lot Like Love* was a hit. People
couldn't get enough of my baby.
[visibly holding back tears]
It was such a beautiful moment for her, to see
that little girl who used to sing and dance in
the living room now living out her dream. It was
something special.

Naomi Wilde
That song stayed on the Billboard chart for like
six months I think.

Interviewer
Seven months, I'm seeing.

Naomi Wilde
Seven? Yeah, okay . . . not surprised!

*With the success of the first single and the hype
for the debut album, record executives and her
new manager were starting to get more involved.
More suggestions about the songs and ideas about
the creative direction and image presented when
it came to her music.*

Martha Fox
The record label wanted her to change. They started
with wanting her to dress a little . . . provoca-
tive.

Naomi Wilde
They wanted her to dress like a slut.

Phoebe Fox
There were so many discussions from different people
at the label or from music video directors. All of
them had different ideas of how or who I should
be for this or that. How to dress, how to wear my
hair, wear more makeup, wear less makeup.

Hanna Chance
I remember at one point someone at Kingdom Records
was pushing for her to get a boob job.

[Video plays of Phoebe at twenty years old, performing in knee-high boots and a sundress as she
paces on stage with her guitar.]

Interviewer
Do you know if at any point Phoebe really considered
altering her body?

Martha Fox
Hell no! Phoebe was smart. She stuck to her guns
with the record label.

Hanna Chance
She wasn't willing to let the machine change her.

Naomi Wilde
They told her that she would need to do something
to sell those records and pretty much put pressure
on her to do what they wanted because they had paid
her already.

Martha Fox
A bunch of damn snakes.

Naomi Wilde
That was honestly my first taste of that. We all
heard stories about that stuff, but we saw it first
hand, well vicariously through Phoebe.

Hanna Chance
They told her sex sells and that she needed to use
it to sell records.

[Video plays of Phoebe in a song circle, singing
while she plays the guitar. Kids around her are
standing up and dancing and everyone is having a
good time.]

Martha Fox
She was singing to kids! Little girls were singing

her songs! You see any interviews on TV and there is a swarm of people, most of them were little girls. You're telling me that sex sells to those fans? The ones that aren't even teenagers yet?

Phoebe Fox
I was told to have my breasts enlarged, I said no. Then they offered to pay for it. Still . . . no. Then it was about me wearing skimpier and skimpier clothes. I'm not against what they are wanting to do to sell records, it's just not who I ever presented myself as when they agreed to sign me. Why would I change now?

Hanna Chance
Phoebe scoffed at the idea and flat out told them multiple times that she wasn't that person and that that's not who they signed when they heard her music.

Naomi Wilde
You know what's wild about all of this? All those men, sitting in their offices, they all tried to coerce Phoebe to do these wild things to herself for attention. Even without all of that, though, she still managed to amass this fanbase. Cover bands dedicate entire sets to Phoebe Fox music. Lookalikes like Aimee on Instagram. What's her name? Do you know who I'm talking about?

Interviewer
Yeah, she's really good at impersonating.

Naomi Wilde
Doesn't she sing too?

Interviewer
I think so, yeah. Might not be as good, but . . .

Naomi Wilde
Right! Well . . . I mean, let's keep it real, who
is?

Interviewer
Fair enough.

Naomi Wilde
Okay . . . So anyway . . . Her second single drops,
this is a month before her album hits stores, and
it's a flop.

Martha Fox
Her song *Dancing Underneath the Porchlight*, a super
catchy love song, got a video, but for whatever
reason it didn't get the same love as the other
song.

Hanna Chance
The record label basically retaliated to her refus-
ing to change her look. They didn't push her video
and the song wasn't spinning on radio stations.

[The video plays from *Dancing Underneath the Porchlight*.]

Naomi Wilde

That video had no budget at all. She had to get real creative with a videographer and even then it was only her on the video. It just wasn't the same as the first. It sort of felt like all of her eggs were in one basket.

Phoebe Fox

They started to be really petty about the deal. They said I wasn't holding up my end of the deal. My manager told me I was being difficult and I didn't think so. I was given an ultimatum to meet them halfway or they would actively invest their money in other artists and if I wanted to do anything I'd have to do it myself. So I did. I hired a videographer and we made a respectable second video, but it never got any traction, not compared to the first song.

Martha Fox

You got this first song, it's still playing on the radio, and then this second song comes out and it's arguably a better song for radio . . . and crickets.

Phoebe's album would debut and still manage to do well in its first week. This changed the attitude from the record label at the time but that was just

*the first red flag for a rocky partnership moving
forward.*

[Video plays from social media of a young girl
holding Phoebe Fox's debut CD outside of a record
store.]

*Flash forward and Phoebe has released four records
and seen substantial growth in seven years.*

[Cut to a teenager who has an entire collection of
Phoebe Fox records and merchandise in her bedroom.]

*Two arena tours and a stadium tour have all but
cemented her as a pop culture icon. The record
label was able to salvage their relationship, but
the friction was always there. Phoebe seemed to
compromise at times with her presentation but never
at the cost of being true to herself. Something she
would become cherished for by her fans. Phoebe Fox
had not only become a juggernaut in all of music,
but she was simply undeniable.*

                    Interviewer
        What can you tell me about Wayne Silverman?

                    Martha Fox
      [Glares at the person asking. Seething.] Wayne
    Silverman is . . . he is just not a good person.
     His heart was made rotten a long long time ago.

Interviewer
And what makes you say that about him in particular?

Martha Fox
You know when you hear people talk about lawyers
and shady businessmen? How they're the worst kind
of people in Hollywood and all that? This is the
kind of person that they mean.

*When Phoebe Fox's multi-album deal was satisfied
there was an overwhelming assumption that she would
leave Kingdom and sign a new deal with someone
new. That idea was never made public, although any
plans she may have had were halted pretty quickly.*

Naomi Wilde
So I wasn't as close with her at this time, but
from what I understand . . . someone had sold the
rights to all of the music at Kingdom Records.
That included Phoebe Fox.

Martha Fox
Wayne Silverman was the manager of another singer
that had publicly tried to ruin Phoebe's name and
made a game of it. She was under attack and it
seemed like everyone hated her. This bad man was
smiling and riding shotgun through it all. A real
piece of work. And a dirty *dirty* old man.

Naomi Wilde

Wayne Silverman bought Phoebe's catalog and the
problem with this was that Phoebe was never given
the opportunity to buy her own music. And now one
of her enemies owned her basically.

Hanna Chance

It seemed like every man in the business just wanted
a piece of her. It was just unethical. She called
me up so angry and told me what was going on.

Martha Fox

I couldn't believe it . . . How is that allowed?
You know?

Naomi Wilde

That set a fire under her.

*It was at this time that Phoebe became a ghost. All
of her social media was wiped clean and no one could
reach her. There was no shortage of theories or
presumptions during her long absence, but it would
seem she was laying low and licking her wounds.*

Naomi Wilde

I remember talking to her when she sort of fell off
the face of the earth for a while. We talked a
little and something in her snapped. You could hear
it in her voice. She was just . . . done.

Martha Fox

She was down, but she wasn't out. This is Phoebe
Fox. This is my little darling. She wasn't the
scared little girl, nervous on stage at the mall
singing for a few dozen people anymore. This was a
bonafide superstar with a voice that she used for
love and positivity . . . until she found a way to
use it to punch back.

[Video plays of Phoebe in black and white with her
head low and eyes dark. She looks up into the camera
in slow motion with a dramatic look.]

Hanna Chance

This is Phoebe Fox. You think she's just going to
go away when the world is still singing her songs
and screaming her name?

*She would go on to stay out of the spotlight for a
while.*

She disappeared from social media . . . vanished.

*It was widely presumed she was off somewhere licking
her wounds.*

*It would be eight months later when the news came
out of her next move . . .*

18

Come on Phoebe, what's the plan, what's the plan? I race to the door and pull it open. Before I even pop my head out I can hear the heavy footfalls approaching. Busy feet charging down the hallway growing louder with each step. I'm positive someone heard all the shouting so I'm not surprised at all. I leave the door open and hide behind it. The bonesaw handle overlaps my knuckles and I hold it like a knife.

How many more people have to die for me to live?

One man comes inside with a rifle drawn. It's one of the two men that was run off by the dead man across the room not too long ago. Their orders are not to shoot me so I react with confidence. As he steps inside, I slam the door shut, and he spins around with a startled expression on his face. The gun misses me and my strike—like a reflex—finds the bonesaw plunged inches into his ear. I scream as I rip it out. I feel the temperature rising in my cheeks and he surely sees the fire in my eyes.

My voice is fierce.

Primal.

Everything that says I'm not going down easy.

The man covers his ear and screams in a higher pitch than my own and the blood flings as I rip it out. The floor catches his body while his legs give out as he whimpers. I should be disgusted with myself but everything leading up until now has been nothing but men telling me what I can and can't do. From unethical business practices in the music industry to what I should or shouldn't say from journalists or other influencers. And now, men with guns who think they can just take whatever they want and put a price tag on it.

I am not a product.

I'm no one's prisoner.

I'm Phoebe fucking Fox.

I walk over to him and shove the business end of the tool into his chest, right where his heart is. My eyes bore into his while I scream behind gritting teeth. The ferocity I feel is only matched by the fear he shows.

I must be too caught up in this small victory because I feel myself ripped away from him and thrown across the room and I didn't even hear the door open. I hit one of the tables and bounce off it and land on the floor. The wind completely knocked out of me. I hold my back and feel where there will no doubt be a bruise after all of this. I don't know how much more I can get my ass handed to me and keep getting back up.

I roll onto my side and see the other guard standing not far from me. An involuntary groan escapes me and I notice the man seeing the other American across the room. He turns back to me, shaking his head in disgust. "Stupid fucking Americans."

I prop myself up on my forearm to get up and I'm corrected by a proper boot to the chest. The wind is forced out of me as I'm sent back to the floor, with authority. I cling to the floor, desperate to scurry away from his towering presence. "Stop!" I beg. He steps over me with his rifle clutched like a ball bat, looking down on me with it cocked back.

The butt of the gun kisses my forehead, but there's nothing sweet about it as my head rocks back and slams into the unforgiving hard floor. I've heard the expression *seeing stars* many times in my life, and I imagine that's what this is. The lights suddenly violate my eyes when they open again and my brain feels like it's sliding around inside my skull and begging for Tylenol. His voice says words that my ears don't receive as everything sounds distant and muffled. Is this what a concussion feels like?

He pulls me off the floor in a violent move that brings me to my feet instantly. I'm light as a feather to this man. His hand finds my throat and he shoves me against a stretcher. We make a lot of noise with sporadic motion as the wheels aren't braked and he applies more pressure, squeezing my neck with a grip that threatens to end me. My hands grab and smack at his arm and I fight to resist him but his strength is overwhelming—his arms are tight as leather with muscles solid like tree limbs. More pressure makes it harder to breathe as he pulls me away from the stretcher and slams me back down against it. Hard.

My hands scratch and claw more at his arms and his other hand fights to restrain my arms. His palm squeezing one of my wrists is a reminder of the bruising and bleeding from the zip tie earlier. With one hand still fighting, I dig my fingernails into his flesh and that causes him to let go.

His face hardens as his brow lowers. His eyes lock onto me the way a cat does when it's hunting. "You bitch!"

I collect myself enough to stand and he slaps me harder than I've ever been slapped in my life. I hit the floor still feeling the sound knocked out of my ear from his massive hand colliding with the side of my head. The ringing sound that follows is more disorienting than the actual contact.

I feel his meaty hands grab one of my ankles and I seize the stretcher to make his intent that much more difficult.

"Come on!" he yells, tugging on my leg. The stretcher comes with me and he tugs again as the stretcher bangs into a stationary table.

With my free leg, I get enough room to pull it and kick his groin, causing him to immediately release me. He drops his rifle before he drops to his knees, covering himself before I can kick him again. I see the blood and heat fill his face and I'm frightened as I watch the hard steel-eyed look of a man become that of a fragile and wincing child.

I get to my feet quickly and the look in his eyes becomes more intense with him scuffling, trying to gather himself and catch his breath while also reaching for me. I remember my brother once told me when we were kids that getting hit there feels like having your testicles sucked up into your stomach. I remember us wrestling and he was tickling me and I accidentally hit him there and he crumbled in a hurry and stopped playing altogether. I remember thinking at the time that it was like hitting a *stop* button. Not much different from now.

As the massive mountain of muscles reaches for me—and misses—he catches himself from falling on his face while holding onto his balls and catching a hand on the underside of the stretcher.

"Oh, you're fucking dead now," he says through pained words with a flimsy threat.

I take a careful step back and as he tries to pull himself to his feet using the stretcher, I hit the bright red handle that looks like a safety release in my clear view. I snatch the end of the stretcher to pull it out from him and as I do, I grab that red handle to get the best grip. When I do, it lifts up and in a blink of an eye the entire bed lowers, slamming down and it's followed by an instantaneous squeal that fills the room. Not that of a man, but more akin to an animal trapped in a snare. But those screams and how his legs slither across the floor make it seem more like a bear trap.

His hand gets caught in the collapsible hinge when I pull the red safety release and the weight of the bed is now crushing and pinching him. Realizing what is happening parallel to the pitch of his pain-ridden cries, I jump onto the lowered bed. His eyes protrude from his head on impact. I stomp again with both feet, harder the second time and he's not faking any reaction anymore. He isn't a tough guy as he starts to cry. With every time I jump it produces more tears and screams from him, and with every scream comes a little more hope for me.

The third stomp echoes the one before it, and so does the fourth and fifth before his shoulder pulls back and rips his hand away from the collapsed stretcher. He falls away holding his hand up and staring at it. The bloody and mangled mess of his hand and disfigured—and disjointed—fingers make me cringe. I have to take advantage of this opportunity. He isn't worried about me anymore. Not with his hand turned into a bruised and pulpy sack of skin with busted bones inside it. I waste no time going for the rifle on the floor that sits behind him.

He's distracted, but aware enough to know I'm going for the gun. As he turns around to look at me, I'm already holding the barrel in both hands with it cocked back like a baseball bat right as I scream and swing. The butt of the gun—the same one he hit me in the face with moments ago—smacks against his cheek and the light in his eyes dim when he topples over to the ground. He rocks, trying to shake it off and as his hand lies on the floor I stand on it, really digging in the ball of my bare foot with a heavy twist.

He screams and submits instantly. "Please, please, stop. I'm sorry. Let go. I can just act like I no saw you and–"

I screw my foot down, feeling how his knuckles mash against the heel of my foot, breaking his words along with his bones while he pleads for mercy. I've never been a violent person, or particularly mean, but I find great satisfaction in a strong oppressor crumbling so easily once the tables turn and they're the ones that are vulnerable.

He looks up at me with his battered hand under my foot.

Pathetic.

His lip shakes while he waits for me to grant him mercy and walk away, but today I am a changed woman. That girl who played the guitar and became a star, and role model to women for all the right reasons is not here. Now, the strong woman who fights for independence, fights for survival, and fights to sing another song for another day stands with this sombering mess of a man at her feet, begging to be spared. I let the moment simmer as our eyes wait for each other to make the next move.

"Where was your mercy when I needed it?" I ask as I raise the gun over my head and bring it down onto his head, like an ax splitting wood as I split his skull with the raining blow. His eyes go out completely, like they were unplugged after just the one hit and he falls over. I kick his hand away and brace myself with a wide stance as I raise the gun over my head, this time screaming as I bring it down on the side of his head again. Blood splashes on impact, but he doesn't react to the second hit. He lies still and quiet as my heart races in my chest. My blood boils and I feel it in my face, realizing how exhausted I am now.

I'm panting. My chest rising and falling and the smell of sweat makes me only want fresh air. The second I get outside I'm looking forward to just feeling the air against my skin and the sun on my face.

I look down at my feet and see the blood and dirt. The bruising. The injuries on my wrists that ride up my forearm. Shades of bruising that sit under the skin and look like watercolors clashing on paper. The gun in my hand is heavy. I turn it over and look at it and see where it's bent—no doubt from me beating a man to death with it.

When I was in high school we once did an exercise in a creative writing course where we were asked to write about where we saw ourselves in ten years. I can guarantee you that this was not it.

L ooking around the room I try to put together a new escape plan. It seems like everytime I get a bright idea, someone else dies.

I take in the mess around me. Tables cleared of their items, now scattered among the floor. Two stretchers against the wall. The radio still plays at an easy to ignore volume. Three men lay dead through-out the room. The amount of blood in here makes me want to retch but something in me takes over and isn't allowing me to respond that way. I look at the heavy-set American slumped against the wall and then the man I just put down. I turn to see the other man, much smaller, lying on the floor. I go over to him and I set the busted rifle on the table as I look at this man and really study his size. He is about my height I notice. I stare at my feet and then his and I think about how much sense it would make to have proper footwear on if I'm outside and need to sprint. I don't know what the environment outside is like or where I am even at.

I sit beside the fallen patrolmen and I start to undo his laces and quickly pull off his boots. I shimmy my foot into one of the boots and stop as I recall a saying I once heard. It's bad luck to wear the shoes of a dead man. There's no time to be concerned about superstitions when my luck is bad enough right now. I shove my foot in and wiggle it to see how loose it is. It's big, but not as bad as I expected. I put on the other one and tighten the laces. I think about how under *normal* circumstances I'd insist on socks, but I can suffer through the blisters after getting out of here.

I stand and try them out, pacing around for a moment before settling on leaving with them. I look ridiculous in this bloodied yellow stage outfit and what are essentially hiking boots. I study the now shoeless man and finagle his pistol from his waist admiring it. I wish I knew more about guns and how to use them. This one seems to be similar to the one I had in the hallway. The one I emptied and tossed. I check the safety and turn it off . . . no need for that.

The boots feel heavy and awkward with every step but I figure I'll get used to them as I walk. I make my way to the door and pop my head out. I lead with pause, listening for pursuant footsteps that might be searching for me. At what point do they lock this place down and send in the calvary? Is there a calvary? I feel the chills through my body at the realization of my ignorance to this place. I don't really know anything at all. I step out with the gun in my palm, hoping like hell there is one in the chamber if I need to squeeze the trigger.

The silence only amplifies the lingering ring in my ear from being hit so hard. I feel the headache whispering with the little throbbing pain behind my eyes. I take steps into the hallway, keeping close to the wall.

The main hallway is clear as I peek around the corner. The only thing I see is where the racking I pulled down during the chase was picked up. The items that were once on it though are still scattered on the floor and strewn about.

I watch every door as I creep past them, expecting someone to come out and try to take me down. I pass the room I was held in and feel the anger bubble up just before the nerves rid me of it.

I'm heading into the end of a long hallway I haven't yet seen, and it feels longer with each step into the unknown. The glow from the outdated light fixtures really showcases how gray everything is. More doors to my left and right and finally I reach the end of the corridor where I'm met with two choices. I can go left where there is a door at the end of a short hall, or I can go right with the same set up. I choose left where there are rooms that branch off but I don't bother with those doors, assuming they're only trouble. I jiggle the handle of the door on the end, hoping for an exit only for it to be locked and holding firm to that promise.

Wasting no time at all, I shuffle to the opposite end and try that one and it also rejects my attempts to turn the handle. I hesitate, listening to the eerie silence, anxious that someone is going to come for me any second. I can't be out in the open in a dead end. The pale gray walls and dirty floors make me feel even more filthy as I deliberate on what to do.

I go back into the main corridor where I'm more visible and I start looking into the tiny windows of the heavy doors. I assumed when passing these at first that they were all just torture rooms. As I study them more, I notice that many of them have signs on the placard, much like a hospital room, only noting them as *Studio A, Studio B,* etc. Now I'm paying closer attention to the rooms without the studio names and near the middle of the hall I find one that says *Production.* I turn the handle and make my way inside and it's dark. I step in, feeling around the wall for a light and find it with ease and I'm standing in an open and familiar space. Wooden floors and vanity lighting. This is where I was cleaned up and that woman acted like I was the star of the show.

The room is clean now, whereas before there were people hustling like some big production. I make my stride across the room toward the door opposite me and I catch my reflection in one of the mirrors, pausing to really see myself. It's hard not to see myself as a monster knowing what I've done here. I see how the blood has dried and ruined the outfit I was forced into. My hair is a mess, my face is bruised, and my body has been through hell. I pull in a deep breath and recognize this monster . . . the one they created.

I stare at the salon chairs lined in a row of four and the uniform mirrors with matching lights at each station. A pair of sinks, side by side, hang from the opposite wall. The rolling clothing racks with various outfits and all of the makings of a typical backstage area.

"Vell, there you are, Miss Fox!" a deep voice says, coming from the French man in the military garb. "You've managed to make quite z'mess for yourself, haven't you?" I stand, frozen, like a child caught stealing. The man paces out of a dark corner and blocks my path. I could turn and run, but I don't know what's waiting for me back there if I do.

"I've only done what you all made me do."

He looks at the floor, snickering before he looks at the ceiling lights with a sigh. "Ah, z'thing now is," he starts, walking toward me as he rotates his wrists and cracks his neck. "You've left me no choice but to stop you by any means z'necessary."

I stagger backward as his feet come at me quickly. The look on his face and stature of his body match the malice in his words. He plans to kill me if he has to. I could never leave and he plans to make sure I don't. "Get back!" I order, raising the gun, taking aim and ready to shoot. Before I can even give him time to feel my threat, he side steps and rushes me, tackling me to the ground.

We knock into a bar table on our way to the floor and it makes a lot of noise. A barstool tips over and every bone in my body lights up in pain as I pound against the concrete. The gun is knocked loose and out of reach and now he is trying to secure my arms. I flail wildly, doing everything I can to keep him from restraining me.

"Get off of me! Get off! Stop!"

I buck my hips to try and break free from him on top of me. I feel his legs tighten and make it difficult for me to continue. He manages to get a hold of one of my wrists. The tenderness is excruciating against his rough and violent touch.

"Stop z'moving! Stay! Stupid girl!" As he fights to secure my arm I sneak a punch into his face. His nose begins to pour immediately and he lets me go. "Ah, verdammte Schlampe!" he shouts.

I'm not sure what he said, but he's clearly pissed off while he blocks the crimson stream from his nose. He reaches his fist back and I flinch as he drives a right hook into my face. I blink hard and slowly and as I open my eyes and watch him reaching for the knocked over barstool. With him reaching away, I happen to see he has a handgun in a holster on his waist. I reach for the gun and he pulls the barstool on top of my chest and leans forward with all of his weight. He screams in my face and all his rage is in his expression, spilling onto me. He doesn't realize I've pulled his gun out of his holster and I raise it to his side, struggling to keep a grip as I fight against him pressing into my chest and collarbone. I feel like I could snap in half any second from the intense pressure.

I curl my finger around the trigger and press the barrel against him and for only a moment, he must realize what I'm doing because he lets up to look at what I have. That little relief is enough to give me that boost of strength as I squeeze.

POP!

He groans, instantly trying to stand, holding onto the area I just shot looking down at me as I'm scrambling to get my feet underneath me and moving. I keep the pistol aimed.

"You . . . you shoot me?" he asks, looking as shocked as I am.

I open my mouth and try to move my jaw around, still feeling the cold from his fist in my sore face. He lunges at me and without hesitation I squeeze again, flinching at the sound of another gunshot. He tumbles over, knocking his head into the sink with a sound that you can only feel. Holding his chest as he rolls onto his back, his chest rises and falls quickly. He looks frantic. No longer concerned with me.

He stares at the ceiling, bleeding from the side of his head now.

I stand beside him and just watch him bleed onto the floor. It only lasts a few moments before his expression dissolves and his head lulls to the side. His breathing stops entirely and I take a moment to collect myself. I place the gun onto the vanity counter and pick up the one I had before the altercation.

I look at the door that's opposite of the one I came in through. The one he blocked me from going to. I move cautiously toward it and notice there's a sign beside it.

Gallery.

Cafeteria.

Service Elevator.

Archives.

20

I open the door and realize it's not as heavy as all the ones before. Two folding chairs sit open with a small table between them. A deck of playing cards and a radio lay unbothered. A metal door is to my left and has a placard beside it. *Cafeteria. Archives.*

To the right, another door just like the other. The placard beside it says *Service Elevator* and *Gallery.* I press on the push bar and stumble into a very long hallway tunnel. Lights are scattered across the ceiling every fifteen or twenty feet maybe with orange extension cords hanging slack connected from one to the next. The echo from the door slamming behind me only makes this hallway feel that much bigger. I walk through the hallway, the walls feeling cavernous. The walkway goes on for a while and many other hallways branch off the sides like interconnected veins.

Signs hang with arrows pointing. I'm following the one that says *Gallery.* I guess I couldn't be lucky enough to find one that says *Exit.* How many people have gotten lost in these tunnels? Many of the ones branching off have no lights, just deep blackness for as long as I can see. I try not to stare down those corridors. I know my brain and I'm already freaked out enough, no sense in working myself up into wondering what's beyond the outreaches of those dark voids.

The air is chilling in here, like I can feeling the creeping darkness grabbing hold of my bones under the manufactured lights. I come to the end where a criss-crossing metal accordion gate waits for me. Another placard hangs saying *Gallery* with a hand drawn arrow pointing up. An old service elevator sits behind the gate as I undo the latch and slide it open. The metal scrapes against the ground while the opening metal squeals and I recall the sound of being brought here. My heavy tired feet step onto the platform of the lift and I see two buttons, one with an up arrow and the other with a down arrow, both drawn on crudely with a black sharpie it looks like. Below them is a slightly larger red button with a white circle and line drawn through it. I'm guessing it's an emergency stop button.

I pull the gate closed, enduring the screeching against the floor as I secure the latch. I stare out into the expansive depth of the hallway I just traversed. What am I doing? I don't even know where I'm going right now. I look down, focusing on the drying blood that's ruined this outfit. Blood from so many men that led me here.

I can't turn back, not now.

I have to keep moving.

Not knowing what's waiting above terrifies me, but the weight of the gun in my hand reminds me that I'm not so helpless anymore. The gun makes me feel strong, even if that's just a fabrication I tell myself. I press the *up* button and a humming sound fills the crevice and the lift shakes before it begins its ascent.

The ride isn't long at all and the lift comes to a slow grinding halt. The humming and vibration stops and I unlatch the gate. I step off the service elevator and the hallway up here is much more normal and less like a hollowed out cave. Actual ceiling lights—much nicer than anything I had seen down below. I make slow strides toward the only door at the end of the short hall, turning the doorknob slowly, easing the door open. I peak through, only a small room greets me on the other side. A couple of fancier chairs than what was down below sit with a small desk and computer monitor, accompanied by an ashtray and open energy drink cans forgotten.

I turn on the light, the walls are painted white and very quickly I notice something odd. There is no door or exit besides the way I came in from, but after looking around for just a moment, I find a suspicious seam in the wall. It's like someone had hung drywall but didn't plaster it to make it look like one complete wall.

I stand closer to further inspect the straight vertical seam that runs from floor to ceiling and as I study it I can hear the rhythm and beat of music.

Bass notes.

I press my ear to the wall and it's definitely directly on the other side of this wall. I lean against it to try and hear better and my feet trip over themselves as I fall forward and the music grows immediately louder. Bright lights flood in and startle me. I catch my balance quickly and I'm standing in a larger, much more open room.

I look back and a massive painting hangs on the other side of the wall that I see now was a makeshift door. That makes more sense. This is a hidden entrance! I feel like I'm in a movie or somewhere I've only heard about on TV or in books. I stand around, astounded and the uptempo music thrums. The bass finds my heartbeat through the floor, pulsing through my legs, and suddenly I feel like I'm on stage with my band again. The lights are changing from color to color. Reds, purples, pinks, blues, greens, all spinning around and transitioning to the music in a coordinated dance of the color wheel.

People stand around in suits, cocktail dresses, and varying degrees of dress clothes as they hold drinks, blow clouds of smoke, and chat lively amongst themselves. No one seems to have noticed me yet.

Who are these people? Are these the people who were bidding on me?

I see large windows that reveal the outside and my hopeful salvation. The night sky spells freedom as far as I'm concerned. Between the exit and me scattered among the open floor are large display cases that people are standing around and admiring. It's hard to see from here but there is some sort of spectacle to what feels like an art exhibit and a night club.

Exhibit.

That's the word that was being thrown around when I first got here. They kept calling me a canvas. Aimee was my artist and . . . is this where she was planning to have me on display?

No one looks familiar, at least not in the strobing and spinning lights. I find my feet moving to the closest display and I walk around and see that someone is on display behind four walls of glass. I try not to react or show the shock on my face when I get a good look. I'm standing within arm's reach of two couples that are already discussing the display.

A man is posed with his head looking to the ceiling as he stands upright, dressed in a tuxedo with the shirt opened and his stomach split open from his chest to his groin.

These people are completely insane. I was supposed to be in one of these display cases. Were people going to idolize the dead celebrity singer while they drink expensive wines and nibble on appetizers? Who is the man in the case with his insides exposed so intentionally? I feel myself staring a little too long and try desperately not to vomit. It's difficult to look at and not feel my stomach clawing its way up the inside of my throat, but I can't look away. The man's intestines are pulled out and fed into his own mouth. Somehow the display isn't messy or bloody. This was cleaned up and staged with the sole purpose to be seen. There's a tag at the base of the glass that has information about the piece. This one is called *Tapeworm.*

"I think that the artist here really had to have a careful hand to do it this well, that's all I'm saying," one of the guys standing nearby says, breaking my intrigue.

"This is just sick, I don't know why you even like this stuff," a woman in a flowy blue gown responds.

"It's not that I like it because it's sick, honey. It's the expression for the profane, don't you see that?" This man asks, wearing a navy blue blazer.

"I get it," another woman, wearing a high ponytail, joins in. "I just don't understand the point of it all. Couldn't you just accomplish this with a painting, like a normal artist?"

"I don't think you do get it, actually," the other man says, adjusting his round-framed *Buddy Holly* style glasses as he finishes the drink in his hand. "Would a *painting* of this make you stop and talk about it?"

The man in the navy blue suit gestures with a smug look on his face. "Thank you! Art is expression. The artist here had to have a careful hand and be delicate, like a motherfucking surgeon with human clay. Restraint. This artist made something beautifully grotesque without letting anger drive their hand. It's simply stunning."

I look away and notice other installations across the floor with people gathered around all sides of them as well. My eyes land on one that I can't really make out clearly from here but it looks like a person with angel wings. My eyes adjust, focusing on it through the changing lights and I realize those wings aren't wings at all. They're made from the skin stretched and peeled off the person's back and still attached.

I can feel the horror wearing on my face with the realization that this is what they had planned for my body. Aimee was going to take my heart, harvest my organs, and then put what was left of me in one of these cases to be gawked at by drunk assholes with too much money. Like I'm some kind of Mr. Potato Head made of flesh and bone or something.

"Oh my God! Are you . . ." the woman in the blue gown says. Her voice catches my attention and suddenly the four chatting about *Tapeworm* here are staring at me with their drinks in their hands and curiosity in their eyes.

"You're Phoebe Fox!" the other woman interrupts, clearly more certain of herself.

"Oh," the man in the glasses says, squinting his eyes and leaning closer to see me. "God damn, hun, you're right. That's Phoebe fucking Fox!"

The man in the navy blue suit looks me up and down and I feel his eyes on the gun in my hand, judging from his nervous expression. "What in the world would Phoebe Fox be doing in a place like this?" he asks.

I'm put off that he didn't address the gun, or the blood I'm soaked in, or the fact that I probably look worse than I feel. Bruised, battered, and beaten to hell. I try to play it cool—whatever that looks like in this scenario.

"Yeah, what are you doing here?" the woman who recognized me asks. "Ooo! Wait, oh my God! Are you . . . are you a part of CAPE?"

I don't know how to answer that. I don't even remember what CAPE stands for. I stare at the four, waiting for whatever is going to happen. I feel my palms clamming up against the handle of this gun as it feels a little heavier and my heart beats faster. Do they know I'm about to escape? Do they know I was just hidden away or even that I've gone missing? They don't seem to know that I was just auctioned off here.

"Oh, wait . . . I get it," the woman with the ponytail says. "I think. Your outfit. I love the grimey look. Like you're coming up from poverty and squalor."

I can see the irony here, as someone who has a lot of wealth, but I recognize right now that I am not *that* kind of rich person. These people are so pretentious and really reaching for a statement of any kind in anything they deem as artistic. What the hell is this lady actually talking about?

"Yeah, okay," her partner in glasses says, nodding along. "Yeah, I see it. The work boots. Those are like a statement that you're not afraid to work hard for the life you deserve. This is powerful. Great work! Who did you work with for this? I'd love to pick their brain for what inspired them."

If I weren't trying to make my way to the exit and run as fast as I can I'd probably laugh at how ridiculous these people sound.

"I love when The Exhibit throws in these live art installations like this," the woman in the gown adds.

"Yes, yes, it's like a regular ole flash mob without the dancing," the guy in the navy blue suit says.

The glasses guy finishes his drink with a gasp as he pulls the glass from his mouth. "Or like a theme park actor."

"I can't believe they were able to pull you from your tour to do it!" says the ponytail woman.

I think I get it. They're not crazy. They're just stupid. In what world would it make sense for me to make an appearance to some secret art show dressed like this just to entertain a few drunks and ghost my actual stadiums full of fans? Their stupidity is the real lunacy here.

"Wait a sec," navy blue says between taking a drag from a cigarette. "Phoebe Fox is on tour right now. No one seems to be able to stop talking about her. There is no way this is her. This has to be an impersonator or something."

Okay, someone is using their brain.

"Like Elvis? Or Michael Jackson?" the lady in the gown asks.

"I mean, Phoebe Fox is outselling both of those icons. But don't all celebrities worth their salt have lines of wannabes and looka-likes?"

"Oh my God! We're being so rude," the ponytail woman blurts out, looking at me. "This lady has a job to do. She's totally in charac-ter. I'm so sorry. We should let you work. We love what you're doing. Knock 'em dead girl!" She gives a wink as she nurses her drink and her party watches me.

I take the moment to break away, walking through the room with the pistol in hand, hanging at my side. My eyes focus on the windows while I scan for a door in that general direction. I watch for the universal glow of an overhanging exit sign somewhere but the busy colorful lights make it hard to pinpoint anything like that. I pick up the pace to hopefully not be seen again by any curious elitist types with sick interests in mutilation while calling it *art*. As the song changes the lights stop changing and we all are under the glow of red lights. I continue my stride and that's when I hear arguing over the low bass note of the song before it gets going. I look to see the commotion and I'm brought to a stop.

I can't believe it.

Am I actually going crazy?

I got knocked around pretty good and still feel off from fighting. My head is still pounding and the bright lights flashing before aren't helping at all.

But is that Wayne Silverman? Is he arguing with . . . is that . . . Scott? . . . New Guy?

21

Scott is alive. What's he doing here? Why is he arguing with Wayne Silverman? Scott knows all about our past conflict and public spats. He shouldn't have any reason to be here.

"I already did my part! I held up my end of the bargain! Is this how you do business?" Scott asks Wayne. His voice raised in a way unfamiliar to me.

"Listen," says, standing confident and affirming. "I have been above board with everything we discussed. You'll get your money when it's done."

"Wayne, with all due respect, it *is* done. As far as I'm concerned, it's been done and what happens from here on out is not my problem. I don't give a fuck what you do with her now. You wanna stick tulips in her ass and call it a garden, fine, I just want my cut, you know, what was promised to me for delivering. I'm the one risking my neck here."

Wayne steps closer to Scott, several inches taller than him with his steel eyes looking down at him. "You're lucky I don't slit your neck right here. You don't think I'm taking on any risk here? You think I don't have as much to lose here as you do? Who the hell are you when you leave here, anyway?"

"I'm the guy who made this all happen," Scott replies, grimacing through his teeth as he pokes Wayne in the chest. "And don't you forget it, you prick!"

"You're just a loser and you–"

"Fellas, fellas," a man says, stepping between the men as things get heated. Is that the auctioneer? "You two, you have this great party. We have guests. Go, be social. Be merry. Discuss the show. We can hash out the technicals after." He puts his arm around Scott and smiles at him, then looks over at Wayne.

That motherfucker set this all up.

It all makes sense. Scott—the new guy—close enough to protect me and have inside info at all times but not close enough to be trusted, at least not when there's a bigger payday to be had apparently. He was behind the ambush and the rest of the security team being picked off . . . Those were all my friends. I treated them like brothers. I treated *him* like a brother even though I hadn't known him as long. I witnessed the others treat him well. I don't understand.

I'm taken back to the ambush and see Scott, curled up on the floor of the passenger seat. I didn't actually see him get hit and just assumed everyone was gone.

I realize through the earth-shattering revelation under red lights and electronica music that I'm just standing here with my eyes open wide in disbelief. A prisoner to the moment as my jaw hangs open and Scott watches me with surprise on his face.

"Guys," he says, sidestepping to tug on Wayne's sleeve.

Wayne pulls away. "Get your hands off me. This suit costs more than–"

Wayne and the auctioneer notice Scott's gaze focused on me.

I freeze. I don't have a plan . . . just a gun.

"Aimee, dear . . . What are you doing up here?" Wayne asks, pulling up his sleeve to check his wrist watch. "Shouldn't you be busy right about now?"

I don't answer him. Is he really that naive?

"Look at you, honey," he gestures at my outfit. "You're all filthy. You look like you had a great time down there. Please tell me you kept her head."

The auctioneer whistles to someone in the distance. He points to me and then nods his head to me. I guess he thinks he is being slick. I see two men heading over out of the corner of my eye. They move through the crowd of onlookers who are far too caught up in their drinks and hoity-toity art discussion to have any clue. No one else in the crowd has caught onto me yet, but the men who I hoped to not be outed by have done just that. I feel the urge to run tingling in my legs. Wayne approaches me, still thinking I'm his daughter.

He stands in front of me with his smug face, and pompous posture that radiates asshole energy. "Wait a minute . . ."

Wayne's face melts and his eyebrows tighten. The two men approach and they're coming right for me. This is where I die, I just know it. Everything I never got to say to my mom and dad simmers in my mouth. I won't get to tell Ashton how much I love him. Naomi . . . Hanna . . . They'll never know what *actually* happened here. I'll never get to pet Paws McGraw again and I feel the tinge of tears welling up in my eyes. My hand feels tense with the weight of the gun. Wait . . . the gun!

"What have you done? Where's my Aimee?" Wayne asks with a concerned tone that falters in the attempt to sound like an authoritative figure, but more like a protective father.

"Don't worry, Wayne," I say, looking up at him with a grin. "Phoebe's head is just fine." I step back, raise the gun and squeeze the trigger, and one of the men approaching hits the floor. The shot hits his cheek and also makes enough noise to get the party's attention. Everyone's eyes are on me now.

"Is this part of the show?" someone asks over the quieting murmurs. The music stops, but I do not.

The other man approaches and reaches into his jacket and I take a shot at him before he can finish his stride. Wayne flinches at the second loud pop and that guard falls to the floor.

People flee the gallery in a sea of confusion and screams.

"You fucking bitch," Wayne growls as he steps toward me. "I'll fuckin' kill ya, you fucking whore. You're gonna fucking–"

A shot rings out as Wayne staggers back, crashing to the floor holding his chest. I stand with the gun raised, staring through the grime on my face. The room is cleared out and I'm laser focused now on every bullet left saying *fuck you* to whoever catches them. Wayne rolls onto his side clutching his chest, bleeding out. The blood pumps through his hand as he tries to apply pressure that seems to be for nothing. That shade of red ruins his high-end designer suit. I stand over him, watching as he dies and his once hardened face only looks afraid. It's difficult for me to not want to show compassion when I look at a person who needs help, but I don't see a person when I look at Wayne. When I look at him, I only see a monster.

"I should have," he coughs up blood, fighting to speak. "I should have killed you mysel–"

POP!

I . . . Phoebe fucking Fox, look down on him before he can say anything . . . He doesn't deserve a last word.

Wayne splays out and the blood spills out onto the floor as his hand falls away.

"Please," the auctioneer pleads, with his hands raised in front of him. He drops to his knees in his baby blue suit. I'm begging you . .

. I've got kids." His fingers are laced as his face trembles. His powder blue pants darken at his crotch as he pisses himself.

Pathetic.

I stand in front of him, pressing the barrel against his forehead. The power is intoxicating. This man didn't consider how scared I was or who I might have had at home when he arranged for me to be sold to whoever was willing to pay. This man is still trash, regardless of anything he's regretting now.

"What about when I was begging?" I ask, pressing harder against his forehead. "Did my life not matter when you were the one in control? Hmm?"

"I'm sorry, I'm sorry!" he says through a rush of tears.

"That's enough, Phoebe. He's just a lackey. Let him go," Scott says, stepping forward with his empty hands raised. "It's me you want to talk to, right? It's over."

My blood boils at him telling me what's over. I turn to Scott. "And why do *you* get to decide it's over when I'm the one with the gun?"

The auctioneer stands up and tries to grab the gun and I squeeze before he can do anything. The bullet hits his neck and he topples over, clutching his throat. His eyes bulge as he stares a hole through me, bleeding profusely on his nice sports coat. He tries to speak and only blood bubbles from his mouth. No more words from the fast-talking proprietor of human beings.

From the corner of my eye I can see Scott moving. I shift my focus to him. "Oh no. You stop right there!"

He stops once more. "Come on, Phoebe. Are you really gonna kill me?"

I keep the gun aimed on him and look around at the four bodies on the floor already. "After the night I've had, do you really want to take the chance?"

An uncomfortable smirk stretches across his mouth. "Fair enough. Listen, you have to know you aren't going to get away with this, right?"

"Get away with what? Being kidnapped and trafficked to a bunch of psychopaths?"

Scott shakes his head, laughing. "These are the top dogs of an underworld cabal. You think they won't find you?"

"I don't care. It doesn't matter what I think. I can tell you what I didn't think though. I didn't think that my personal security—someone I took care of and treated like family would betray me like you did."

"Phoebe, look . . . it's isn't what it looks like–"

"I fucking heard you just now. Talking to that piece of shit!" I gesture to Wayne's body. "I heard you two bickering, over what? Money?"

Scott closes his eyes. My accusation cutting through him, more like an admission of guilt the longer he's still breathing. "Phoebe. It wasn't personal. This just . . . this wasn't even my idea. Everything got out of hand so quickly." Scott takes another step toward me.

POP!

Scott falls to the ground, grimacing in pain, holding his thigh. The more he speaks, the hotter my face feels.

"What the fuck!?"

"What do you mean, *what the fuck?* I'm not getting out of here anyway, right?"

"Phoebe. Please . . . Let me help you."

"Help me? I think that ship has sailed, *New Guy.*" I never subscribed to rattling his cage like the others when he worked for me by calling him New Guy. But, I know how much it irritates him and I can't resist. He seems more distracted by the hole in his leg to care.

That isn't as satisfying as I hoped it would be, but watching him scoot across the floor is a nice substitute.

"I regret everything. If I could apologize and somehow make it up to you I will. I know you're pissed. I just got caught up in all of this. I didn't even want to initially."

I pause for a moment. "Wait a second . . . You said this wasn't even your idea. What do you mean, Scott?"

He smiles. "I will tell you anything you want if you help me get out of here. You have to promise not to kill me."

"Um, I don't think you're in any position to barter. Did you forget who has the gun?"

Scott laughs. "Well, do what you gotta do then. Kill me if you have to."

I point the gun at his face and we stare at each other. His eyes are just as intense as my own. I'm tired and just want to go home. I'm sick of talking.

I squeeze the trigger.

Click.

Fuck.

Scott exhales and his face lights up with glee. Laughter follows and he props himself up to stand. The laughter becomes obnoxious before he is upright.

"Looks like it's your lucky day." I toss the firearm into one of the art installations and the glass cracks, but doesn't shatter.

Scott falls back over, struggling to stand on the injured leg.

I smirk, turning away to go over to the art display I just damaged. I grab the base that holds the rope and I swing it into the glass to finish the job. It shatters and the profane display inside is of a woman posed with a hammer in her hand and nails decorating her entire body. I pry the hammer from her dead hand, disgusted at how she died. She was likely alive while a lot of those nails were put in her, and probably from this hammer. I walk toward Scott as he is promptly back on his ass, scooting away, leaving streaks of blood on the floor now.

"Hold on, hold on . . . waitwaitwaitwait!"

"I'm sick of waiting. Tell me everything, or it's hammer time. Do you understand?"

"I-I . . . I was approached by someone. They offered to pay big money if I just gave your location and schedule during travel."

"How much?"

"What?"

"How much did they pay you!?"

He looks at the floor, the first time I've seen him look ashamed. "Fifty K."

"You sold me and the others out for fifty grand!?"

"It wasn't my idea, I swear! I didn't even want to."

"I pay you a lot more than that. And I thought we were friends! Is that all our friendship was worth to you!?"

"I didn't know what they had planned. I didn't know the CAPE was this whole super connected underworld thing. I'm so sorry."

"I had plans to give you guys bonuses once this was all over, the tour I mean. I was going to pay you, the other guys, the dancers, the truck drivers, everyone was going to get a hundred grand! . . . What was your actual plan if you got away with this?"

"I don't know! I told you, it wasn't my idea!"

"Whose idea was it then if you aren't the mastermind?"

He stares at me, ready to cry. His chest rising and falling as he continues to bleed from his leg wound. The hesitation hangs between him and I. "Maybe you should talk to your boyfriend."

My heart skips a beat feeling the double whammy of betrayal hit me like a ball peen hammer. It all makes sense now.

"Phoebe?"

No response comes from my mouth, just a primal scream as I swing the hammer, letting it crash into Scott's skull.

I mash and swing, blow after blow. Blood slinging and coming away from him like ropes each time I extract the hammer.

Top of the head.

Temple.

Temple.

Cheek bone.

Temple.

Ear.

Back of the skull.

Forehead.

Nose.

The other cheek bone.

A part of the skull I haven't hit yet.

Again.

One more time.

A new scream expelled with each wild swing as Scott's head bounces off the floor with every impact. The bone collapses, caving under the weight of the hammer every time I feel the shock surging through my palm and knuckles with every hit. And then I stop, leaving the hammer buried in his head.

22

The quiet is almost peaceful. I stand in the front of a gallery with a showcase of horrors that a bunch of rich assholes dare to call *art*.

No more flashing lights that disorient my already throbbing head.

No more loud music that suggests I dance when I know I should be running.

Only silence among the bodies I've left on the floor.

I look at the two guards who I don't know and wonder how long they may have been a part of this. My instinct is to feel bad but part of me can't help but feel like they deserved it somehow. Call it consequences of their line of work, and tonight, I was their consequence.

I look at the auctioneer's body and get angry. The nerve of some men to ignore someone in need—like it's just another day at the office. His pitiful end seems fitting.

And then there's Wayne Silverman. Debaucherous record exec and mogul with a reputation for blacklisting his enemies and wielding his influence around like a giant dick. I'm not surprised that this son of a bitch is involved in this sort of group. I'd heard rumors of these secular elitist groups before, but never knew for sure if they really existed. I always thought they might just be ideas that get the conspiracy theorists talking. Wayne was one of my greatest enemies though and of the lot that died here tonight, he is the one I feel absolutely nothing for. That is considering that he would just as easily see me dead under any circumstances. Paying millions of dollars just so his obsessed psychotic daughter could play doctor with me and rip my heart out for her own is really a lot of effort just to get . . . revenge, I guess?

And then there's Scott. Former employee . . . former protector. Inside man with inside info, travel companion, and once a friend. My heart aches at the reality of him betraying me and the others. Because of him, Jack, Aaron, and Harry are dead, and also an innocent driver. There is no room in my heart for forgiveness for what he's done and my heart bleeds at the weight I have to carry. Knowing that when I make it out of here that I'll have to face their families. I don't have it in me, but I need to get there first, and to do that, I need to get out of here.

I just want to go home and crawl into bed and see my mom. A hug from her sounds like the warmest place on the planet right now. I don't want to say anything, just be with someone I can fully trust and let this all just be a memory. I feel my temperature rising thinking about the one person who I wish I wanted to be with right now, and a fire burns inside of me thinking about seeing him again. Ashton isn't going to get away with this, and I'm committed to making sure he understands just how bad he fucked up.

The media circus about me missing must be nuts right now. It's going to only be more chaotic when they get wind that I've resurfaced. Here I am getting ahead of myself, I need to get out of here. I head toward the front door and see one of the guards and their gun lying visible on the inside of their jacket beside their body.

It might be a good idea to have it—I don't know what's waiting for me outside of this place.

With a new—and unfamiliar—pistol in hand I gravitate to the glass double doors. The night time spills in and as I pause to look out, I see groups of people standing around. All dressed in their designer clothes. Some still with their glasses in hand as they wait for this to play out, like they're still not convinced this is really happening. Like it's all some sort of elaborate showcase of violence. Like I'm that good of an actress. Like there would actually be any kind of point to any of this anyway. I'm anticipating police or more guards at any moment. I'm ready to open fire on anyone who shows even a shred of aggression. I check the pistol for safety and it's not in the same spot. This one is ready to fire, I see the red where the safety is off.

I stand at the doors, one hand on the gun and the other on the push bar where the cool air waits to cling to my skin, and the guests gossip and speculate what I'll do next. Did they watch me with the hammer a few minutes ago? I close my eyes and let the air flow through my body before finally, I push the doors open. They both fly apart and I strut through the threshold in these clunky black boots and this yellow outfit that is hardly even yellow anymore. The sequins still manage to shimmer when I walk out. The moonlight reflects as the crowd watches me like a predator in the wild. The gun in my left hand, like a lioness baring her teeth.

No one moves a muscle.

No one dares to stop me.

I can feel myself in slow motion.

I can hear their whispers before they even start.

They just watch Phoebe Fox controlling her story. I can see their faces, they don't know what they should do other than watch. They're afraid of what I *might* do . . . and I kind of like it that way. Curious eyes follow me nervously as the soft chatter stops. The gravel and dirt crunches beneath each step I take. The sweat on my skin dries against the slight breeze that carries a woodsy scent. As I pass through I catch the curious glances from rattled strangers, waiting for me to put on a show for them.

What song might I sing?

What dance might I do?

Who might I shoot in the face first?

I stop and really scan the gawkers. Well dressed, elitist types. Designer formal wear and petrified expressions that don't pair well with their luxury fits and entitlement. I raise the gun to the crowd, pointing it at no one in particular feeling the unbound rage tear through me.

"Did you all enjoy the show?" I shout, jabbing the gun in their direction. Small gasps crawl through the crowd as the gun moves. The scared and shocked faces of people in attendance cower under my unpredictable brandishing of the weapon. I lower it, feeling the shitty look worn on my face. "Show's over."

A familiar face watches me. Linda Sharpe, a trash TV day-time pop culture host. She knows I recognize her, I know that shameful look on anyone and this woman was always kind to me in front of cameras, but never one to offer much else. I often heard rumors about her playing golf with executive types and big wigs in the entertainment industry, but now it makes sense, seeing her in a place like this. I like watching her sweat. That's right, clutch your pearls, Linda.

I pass the crowd and no one comes chasing me. I'm relieved, but scared to let my guard down just yet. Not with all of those sick fucks at my back, watching me kick rocks up this long driveway through the darkness. The night takes me away from their watch as the bruising on my face begins to throb, reminding me that I've gotten my ass whooped all night. I'm bloody, and I can't differentiate what's mine or someone else's. Thick layers of grime and filth coat my skin as I approach a paved road with The Exhibit at my back, as parody of myself—or a much stronger version.

23

The stars really pop tonight. My feet drag along the cracked and dusty road under a dark sky that teases salvation. Clouds coasting along to the breeze making it look almost like the moon is winking at me. Maybe this is the universe's sick way of telling me tonight was all a joke. If that's the case . . . terrible joke.

There are no streetlights or anything to suggest this is a populated area. Definitely has a rural feel, but I can't see much in the dark. There are trees in the distance and the road goes for as long as I can see. My feet throb and my knees beg for rest at the thought of walking that kind of distance. Nothing about the landscape is recognizable, so my plan is to just keep walking. I'll walk until I can get help or eventually find a town. This road has to lead somewhere.

I wish I knew what time it was. My pace wanes as the fatigue tightens its grip. My heart is no longer racing and all of my bruises start to scream for attention. I walk for what feels like forever. I say that because the dark has begun to lighten up as the black sky peppered with stars becomes a hue of lighter blue that meets a warm and welcoming orange. This view of a new day being born is quite the contrast against the concrete and blood that I just fled. The morning has come and it shines its hopeful light onto the road before me and I maintain my pace, even if it feels more like I'm dragging myself along the road.

I feel each step I take is less predictable with each foot landing. I'm shambling up the road like a monster with a gun in hand. The birds sing in the trees as the sun peeks over the horizon more. From behind me I hear a humming motor in the distance and perk up at the noise like a scared animal. I turn to look and see a car coming up the road toward me. Whoever that is will have to see me. I'm unsure how far I've walked but I know I'm tired of walking. I've waited for someone to pass through and this is the first car I've seen, which tells me that this road is not often traveled.

I step away from the shoulder and into the middle where I can be clearly visible. I'm cautious enough to hide the gun in the waistband of my skirt, stuffing the barrel into the small of my back. A pale blue sedan slows to a stop as a man driving rolls down the window. A young blonde woman sits in the passenger seat and I can feel her eyes judging me. It isn't lost on me how insane I look right now. If it were me, I would probably just keep driving if I were to see a woman dressed like she just stumbled out of a night club covered in blood.

The man sticks his head out the window, shouting something I can't understand.

"I'm sorry," I reply. "I only speak English. Do you speak English?"

The man turns to the girl and as his head is turned I draw the gun and point it at him. I approach his door and his passenger screams, ducking down before he notices. He puts his hands up wearing a confused look on his face.

"I speak English. Take what you want and just let us go!" the woman begs, screaming into the floor of the car.

I study the car and their scared selves and feel a sense of relief. I see backpacks in the back seat and what looks like rolled up sleeping bags. These aren't dangerous people. They can't be. I feel my chest tighten as the guilt of pointing a loaded gun at these—hopeful-ly—innocent people hits me. I can't help but to form assumptions in my mind as I stare at them. They look like a young couple, prob-ably traveling to go camping or hiking somewhere. Maybe they are driving home, or maybe on their way. I imagine the woman having a child, maybe the child is theirs and staying with a family member.

I lower the gun, and raise my hands, offering surrender. "Can you help me?"

The woman raises up and stares at the driver with sad eyes. Words pass back and forth between them as their eyes dart to and from me.

"Please?" I ask, ready to beg, choking back a sob that threatens to break my voice.

The man says something and the woman's eyes linger for a mo-ment, but a moment that feels like forever. "Get in. Leave the gun."

I shudder at the idea of being defenseless but my gut tells me these are decent people. Against safer judgment, I need to know where I'm going and I don't know what lies ahead or how much road awaits. They can very well drive off right now and I'd be back to scraping my feet against the gravel and dirt until I beg the next person in passing. Who knows when that might be though. I need serious help, and medical attention. This may be my best shot.

I keep my hands up as I squat down. I sit the gun on the ground and stand with my hands still raised, backing away a couple paces.

"You get in back," the woman says.

I don't hesitate, shuffling to the door and sliding in. Immediate relief hits me like a crashing wave as my legs thank me. "Thank you so much."

The driver turns off the car and steps out of the vehicle and grabs the gun. He stuffs it in his waistband, looking around before getting back in the car. He starts it up and we're driving. My body sways against every minor movement of the car as music plays.

"Thanks again," I say. "I'm sorry about the gun."

"It's okay. You're safe now."

The man says something to the woman and they go back and forth.

"Where do you need to go? Hospital?"

I consider where. "Can you take me to the airport?"

"Airport?" she asks, surprised.

"I need to get back home."

The man speaks again to the female passenger.

She turns back to look at me. "What happened to you?"

This is what I didn't anticipate. Of course they want to know what my story is.

"I . . . I was taken by some bad people and they tried to kill me."

She stares at me in disbelief. "Who took?"

I stare out the window at the trees whipping by. "It doesn't matter."

I can feel her eyes on me. I can't bring myself to meet her eyes because I might want to share more. This may be a situation where knowing less is best for them. She's putting together her own assumptions in her mind, I just know it. Even more though, does she have any idea who I am? I'm sure my bruised face is working in my favor right now. I really don't want to get into a fan interaction right now. I'd hate for anyone to see me like this. The realization is only just now hitting me that I am going to have to answer to the media about the tour and what happened.

"You need a doctor," she says to me.

"I know. I will see someone at the airport."

She turns back around and she and the driver talk amongst themselves while I fight to not lean my head on the window. I don't want to bleed and dirty up their car anymore than I already have. "He says the airport is a bit away. We take you if you don't go to hospital."

"Thank you."

We arrive at the airport and I sit, planning my next move. Every airport feels the same after you've been to enough of them. I've gotten used to flying private in recent years, but that clearly won't be an option here. "Wait, one second," the woman says. She gets out of the car and opens the door to the backseat and takes one of the backpacks and starts unraveling the contents onto the seat beside me. "You can't go on plane looking like," she gestures a hand up and down at me. She's right though, I'm dressed like a sunflower with questionable stains. She tosses me a cardigan and says something to the driver. I hear the *pop* sound and she goes around to the trunk.

We sit for a moment before she comes back and tosses me a black garment. I have a look and see she is giving me yoga pants.

"I get new. You change here. We won't watch." She tells the driver something and quickly covers his eyes.

"I can repay you when I get back to the states. I really appreciate you. Both of you!" I feel myself wanting to cry but I try my best not to.

"You change." She turns her back to me and leans on the window. I'm quick to slide into the pants and I am glad to take the skirt off. I put the cardigan on and hope no one can see through it or notice the blood.

"I'm done."

The man uncovers his eyes and watches me in the rearview.

"Thank you," I tell him, unsure if he understands me. "I'm sorry that I pulled the gun on you." He smiles at me as I get out of the car and the woman meets me near the trunk.

"Will you be okay?" she asks me.

"I'll be okay," I tell her, not so sure I believe that myself. I offer a hug and she pulls me in.

"I don't know what happened to you . . . but I hope you get help and get back home."

"I will, thank you." We separate and I feel the tears coming. I look at her, a total stranger who just helped me in what is easily the toughest moment of my life and I see her wiping her eyes. "What is your name? How can I repay you?"

"My name is Eline. And you don't have to repay. Just take care of yourself." She grips my hands in hers and we have a moment. Two women who see each other on a human level. No status or cultural divides. Just two people. One in need of help, the other in a position to lend a hand to a stranger.

I hug her one more time. "Thank you, Eline. I wish great things for you and him."

I let her go. She smiles at me and gets back into the car and I watch as they drive away.

24

I stand in the main lobby overwhelmed as I stare at signs that probably tell me where to go, yet I feel like a dumb American standing alone in an international airport. I start walking in hopes to not look like such a lost little girl. An information desk looms nearby and I pass by it when I notice the universal sign outside of a door. The restroom. I go into the ladies room and as I see a stall I realize just how bad I've had to pee this entire time. I sit, staring at my wrists and the remnants of being restrained against my will. Moisture crashes onto my forearm, beginning as only a drop at first, becoming a sobbing mess as I let go. A moment to myself where I'm not hiding or fighting for my life is realized in an airport bathroom stall.

I sit here, the sound of my cries breaking against my chest heaving and bucking uncontrollably. The tears rush down my face and my vulnerabilities are breaking free. I made it. Somehow, I actually made it out alive. All I want to do is talk to my mom right now and just hear her voice. I'm grateful to be sitting on this toilet, behind the comfort of a weak deadbolt lock. I try to pull myself together and that's when the events of The Exhibit really start coming into perspective. I've not had a moment to really consider what all had happened because I was on constant defense.

The man being tortured in the room next to mine.

All of the bad people trying to kill me who I had to kill for me to live.

Why did it have to be this way? I can't even think confidently of how many people are dead—because of me.

My sobbing comes to a pause when I hear the bustle from outside as the door opens and two women wander in chatting. Plastic luggage wheels roll against the tile and I wipe my eyes and face.

Come on, Phoebe. Get yourself together.

Moments pass as I sit here in this stall, deliberating on what I should do from here. I hear people coming in and out of the restroom and the sinks turn on and off before I realize I've sat here for entirely too long.

You're not done yet. You can't fall apart now.

I finish up and head to the sink once I hear the bathroom is empty. I stand in front of the mirror and reflect on the last twenty-four hours as I stare back at myself.

Look at you.

You've overcome so much.

You can do this.

Bruising and swelling decorate my face where my makeup once was and has since run and dried. I turn on the sink, eager to splash warm water on my face and begin cleaning off the dried blood. I use paper towel after paper towel to clean myself up as much as I can. A woman walks in, breezing just past me. I ball up a fistful of the wet, bloody, and soiled paper towels and toss them into the trash hole in the countertop. She pays no attention to me—thankfully. I tousle my hair and try to look as normal as I can, all things considered.

I leave the restroom before the woman has a chance to stand beside me at the sink and possibly recognize me. I'm used to flying private and never stepping foot in an airport so this all feels unfamiliar to me. I can be seen and it turns into a circus, or I can be seen and people don't believe it's me. I'm hoping for the latter. The airport is lively as I make my way to the information desk. There is a short line but I'm not waiting long before I am waved over to an older woman. She greets me with a smile, although I have no idea what she is saying. I can only imagine it is some form of *How may I help you?*

"English?" I ask. She holds up her finger to me to wait a second. She grabs her phone and starts doing something and then speaks into it and shows me the screen. Google translate. Thank God for the age of technology. What a time to be alive.

"How may I help you?" it reads as she hands me the phone.

I hold the button and speak. "I need to speak with police or security, please. In private."

I hand the phone back to her and she listens in her language and looks at me with sad eyes and a friendly smile as she nods. She picks up a phone at her desk and dials, going back and forth with someone for a moment. She hangs up and speaks into her phone and hands it to me again. "Please, have a seat and someone will be with you."

I smile and nod with my hands clasped together in the universal *thank you* gesture. I take a seat and it's less than a minute before a uniformed officer comes out and the woman at the help desk points me out to the man. Clean-shaved with an imposing stature, the officer comes over to me. "You need some help, miss?"

Oh, thank God! Someone who speaks English! "Um, yes. Do you have an office or a place where we can talk in private?"

The thought of a private space with someone sets off every alarm in my mind, but as I observe the airport, and behind the help desk, the many visible cameras offer some semblance of comfort. Maybe a reminder that not everyone wants me dead.

"Of course. Come with me." He gestures his arm to join him. His English isn't perfect but clear enough to have a productive conversation with. He leads me to a door where he waves a security badge to be allowed access. We walk through a corridor of offices before reaching another door requiring access. As we enter, there are several security guards monitoring live surveillance of the airport.

We go into an office that is small, with only a desk and two chairs across from it. "Please, have a seat," he says, as he goes around the desk to sit. We both take our seats and stare at each other. "What can I do for you?"

I don't know where to begin. Maybe I just need to tell him who I am and why I am here. How I got here. I know a million questions will follow. "If I tell you something, it stays confidential, right?"

"Of course."

"Okay," I say. I take a deep breath in preparation to unload onto this officer. "So, I am Phoebe Fox." He stares at me, unmoved, which surprises me. Has he not heard of me? Maybe this is for the best if that is the case. "International pop singer . . . no?"

"I know who you are," he responds, deadpan and professional.

"Okay . . . Well, I am on a huge stadium tour right now and I was kidnapped while traveling from the airport here to my rental."

"Yes, you're all over the TV and internet. Do you know who was responsible?"

Yes. "No, I don't. I managed to get out of there but they were going to kill me."

"Do you know where you were being held?"

"I do not."

"How did you get here?"

"I got a ride from a stranger."

"A stranger?" he asks, suspicious of my answer.

"Yes. I just need to get back to the states. I need to contact my mother to let her know I'm safe but I would like to keep this quiet if we can."

He leans back in his chair with a thoughtful look on his face as the seat groans against his weight. "Okay. I can help you. But you will need to answer some more questions about what happened. I hope that's okay."

"Yeah, yeah, that's fine."

We spent the last hour recapping the events of yesterday and last night before I was given access to a computer. I promptly logged into my email and grabbed my mom's phone number from the contact. I am given privacy and the officer's desk phone as I dial the number and sit here.

As the phone rings I begin to tear up, hoping that she answers.

I fight back the tears after the first ring, but it's on the second when she answers and I feel my heart crash and everything rush out from the inside of me.

Hello?

I can't help but weep into the phone at the sound of my mom's voice. My own voice, incapable of breaking through the ugly cries and breakdown. There was a time when I truly thought I'd never hear her speak again. I'd never have the chance to speak to her again. All of the emotions that come with wondering what she would have thought happened to me if I never were to call her again. I still have no idea what is being said in the world. The internet has a way of painting a blurry picture that the majority of folks will believe blindly.

"Phoebe? Honey . . . is that you?"

I nod my head knowing she can't see me, but it's all I can do right now. My chest is tight and I can feel the redness in my face.

The wave of relief crashing against the realization that this is truly improbable that I'm even alive. How am I even on the phone right now, breathing? It's a miracle that I'm able to cry right now.

"Hello?"

"I'm here, Mom," I manage to say through a hard sob and choking breath.

"Phoebe! Oh Lord, Thank goodness! I have been worried sick!" The pitch of her voice tells me she might break down any second too. "Your assistant called asking if I'd heard from you and I hadn't then I called and called, and then the news started saying these awful things, and–"

"Mom," I interrupt. She's clearly emotional.

"Yeah, baby?"

"I love you." I had to tell her that before anything.

"Oh, I love you too, honey. What's going on? Where are you?"

"I'll tell you everything when I get home, but I need your help."

"Of course. Anything. What do you need?"

"I need you to buy me a plane ticket to New York and then book me a room please."

"Sure. But why not just come home?"

"There is something I need to do first." The less she knows, the better.

"Yeah, yeah, yeah, okay. You need a flight now? From where?"

"Amsterdam Schiphol International Airport."

"Wait, you're in Amsterdam? What about your show? Have you talked to anyone?"

"Listen, Mom!"

"People are freaking out thinking something happened–"

"Mom!"

"Yeah, baby?"

"Something happened, I said I'll tell you. Please don't tell anyone you heard from me though. Keep it quiet until I say, please."

"Oh, I don't know, you know I have a terrible poker face. And people keep calling me and asking if I've heard from you."

"I know. I'm just asking you to keep it quiet for at least a day. I need to take care of one last thing and then I will come up with an announcement for whatever I need to. I'm sorry to put you through this."

She's silent, leaving only the dead air on the phone between us. "Okay," she huffs. "Can I at least meet you in New York?"

"Sure. But the next day please. I need a day."

"Okay. Can I call this number back to let you know I got the tickets and where you're staying?"

"Sure. I will let them know you're calling back."

"Okay. I will try to hurry. I love you."

"I love you too."

We hang up and I sit for a moment, considering what to do next.

Forty minutes pass before my mom calls back and I have the information needed to travel. I worked out how I'm going to do the passport and identification with security. In the time I was waiting for my mom to call back a detective came by asking to speak with me about what happened. Considering that I'm a sitting duck until my flight to New York, it wasn't possible to avoid the detective. I insisted on confidentiality and nothing being leaked to the media at all and he agreed to wait before filing any paperwork officially.

After talking with the detective and bringing him up to speed, he confirms that they found the SUV and my protection . . . my friends, and the local driver. All dead. I explained that my assistant arranged the ride and our flight details from the private plane that flew in from Ireland and once they confirmed those details they were able to arrange safe travel back to the states. The detective told me by this time tomorrow though, my information would be logged officially and that he couldn't guarantee what gets leaked or seen after that. I'm more than thankful for that, but I only have one thing on my mind now. My flight leaving later and an old flame in need of a heart to heart chat.

I sit in the security officer's office. It's been hours now and my flight departs soon. The guard has already arranged for me boarding and getting me onto the plane after everyone else has boarded to help ensure I'm not seen. I can't help but feel lucky.

He opens up a cabinet and pulls out a baseball hat and tosses it to me. "You like the Yankees, yeah?"

"Um, sure."

"You take the hat. To hide your eyes on the plane."

I stare at the NY logo that is so common in sporting gear. "Thank you," I say as I pull the hat onto my head.

I boarded the plane, seated in first class—thank you mama—and security was very considerate—all things considered. For now, everything feels somewhat normal again and as the flight leaves the ground and we head for the United States. I try to keep the bill of my hat low in hopes that no one will recognize me and so far no one has spoken to me or given me reason to think they know who I am.

My hands sit in my lap and I slip my fingers underneath the beads of the friendship bracelet that hugs my bruised wrist.

Strong Enough.

I'm reminded not only of those two beautiful girls in Ireland that I exchanged bracelets with, but also of the promise I made to them. I have a song to sing and a responsibility to make sure they get to hear me dedicate a song to them on stage. Everything I went through, I survived.

I'm still here.

I owe it to those girls who are fighting for their lives every second to keep that promise.

I feel my tired eyes closing as everything goes quiet. I settle in, getting comfortable as the peacefulness overtakes me.

<u>**The Rise of Phoebe Fox [Documentary] Part 4**</u>

*With old enemies getting the upper hand on Phoebe
by owning her music, she felt betrayed. Her label
manager not allowing her the opportunity to buy her
masters before the merger was a sign of disrespect
and one she wouldn't forget.*

[A video montage plays of Wayne Silverman and others
having a good time. Phoebe Fox walking with shades
on as paparazzi cameras flash.]

Martha Fox

When that all happened, yeah, sure, they bought her
music and publishing, but to that little girl with
a dream . . . she felt like they were buying her.
Like they owned her.

[A man takes a seat across a table at a quiet cafe.
Baristas are busy behind the counter out of focus
behind him. The name is displayed at the bottom of
the screen. Ashton Craig, Music Journalist.]

Ashton Craig

Phoebe and I had always had a friendly relationship.
When she was off the grid, so to speak, we spent
some time together. She was really hurt by what had
happened and just the two-faced nature of it all.

Interviewer
Do you know what ultimately led her to the big
announcement?

Ashton Craig
Which one? The re-recordings?

Interviewer
Yeah. That is something that hadn't really been
done, at least not at the scale that she had done
it.

Ashton Craig
I believe we were holed up in a hotel somewhere when
she got on a rant and just was riffing and drinking
wine. She threw out the idea and it sounded absurd
at first. There was a cheekiness to it, between
swigs and all. The more she talked it through out
loud though, the more it really made sense and the
more serious she sounded.

Phoebe Fox
It made perfect sense. While I was busy being sad
and feeling sorry for myself, one night it just
kind of hit me. I was literally doing nothing
else creatively. I started looking into publishing
rights and recording masters to see if I could
realistically do it and what do you know? I sure
can!

Naomi Wilde

Phoebe had started rerecording all of her albums that Kingdom had once owned, and now Wayne Silverman owned.

Martha Fox

She planned to own her music again, and if that monster wasn't going to sell her music back to her then she would find a way.

Naomi Wilde
[Laughing]

Can you believe, Silverman called it an "investment" when he publicly refused to sell her the rights back. That wasn't an investment, that was a tactic. A tactic that felt like a middle finger with a smile to match.

Phoebe Fox would quietly spend the better part of a year rerecording her music. It would sound as close to the original as possible and in some cases, maybe even better.

Ashton Craig

It was crazy. She came out of hiding and showed up on a talk show to announce what she was up to.

[Video plays of Phoebe on a daytime talk show, smiling through an interview.]

                    Martha Fox
Her fans went nuts! They missed her, you could tell.

[Video montage plays of young fans on camera excited
about the announcement. Cut to fans lined up outside
of a Target.]

                    Naomi Wilde
I think people were ready for more of her. She
dropped that bomb and was instantly trending every-
                       where.

                    Hanna Chance
Front page articles, newspapers, websites, magazines. The world couldn't get enough of her.

                    Phoebe Fox
All of a sudden this crazy idea turned into every
news outlet, radio station, podcast, all wanting
to talk to me. Where was this treatment when I was
with Kingdom records? It's not like the songs are
different. It's the same music that everyone has
                    heard already.

                    Ashton Craig
It was a sight to behold, truly. Her fans were like
a military unit, awaiting her command. When she
told them that supporting her music then was only
making Silverman richer, it was like nothing I had
ever seen. A majority of them stopped streaming the
music. There is actual data from Apple, Spotify,

Youtube where you can see the dip from the day of
that announcement. An immediate response.

Naomi Wilde
Oh, Phoebe's fans are *serious* serious. They don't
play . . . and they showed up for her and let their
time and money talk.

Martha Fox
When the first rerecorded version came out,
Phoebe's Cut, fans were all over it. Social media
had hashtags and things only blew up from there.

Hanna Chance
You thought she was a pop cultural phenomenon before
the Phoebe Cuts?
[Shakes head with wide eyes.]
Her fans are some of the most loyal and supportive
fans anyone in the world could have.

[Cut to videos from fans speaking in a series of
news interviews]

Field Reporter: What is it about Phoebe Fox that
makes you a fan?

Young Girl: Her music, it's like she is writing the
soundtrack to my life, what I'm feeling. Anytime
I'm feeling anything I think, there is a song for
that. Phoebe has a song for that.

[Cut to a different person]

Field Reporter: What is it about Phoebe Fox that makes you willing to spend your money on an album you've already heard before?

Young Woman: It's not so much the music that we're supporting. We're supporting independence. She was taken advantage of by a bad man and at the end of the day money talks. She's always been so good to us fans and she has always kept it real and honest and, to me, it's a no brainer that I would support her. I let my dollars speak against misogyny and oppression.

This act was more than Phoebe just wanting what was hers. This was a line in the sand against men like Wayne Silverman.

[Cut to clip from a previous interview with Wayne Silverman walking outside]

Wayne Silverman: You know, it was bad enough that she slandered my name and has her little teeny-boppers sending my family death threats, but her taking action to rerecord all of that music is bad business from her and her team. What is the point in owning the publishing rights to something if the artists are just going to be allowed to

copy it and redistribute? It's absurd. It's
f***ing absurd!

Field Reporter: You've received death threats?

Wayne Silverman: Yes! You know, and I understand
she is angry and feels however she feels, but
at the end of the day this is just business and
nothing personal. She made it personal and then
continues to allow her fans to contact my family
and say horrific things to my wife and kids.

Field Reporter: What would you have Phoebe do if
you could talk to her?

Wayne Silverman: Talk? . . . That woman doesn't
want to talk. And if she can't put two and
two together to call off her fans then she
is no better than them by letting it happen.
Unprofessional, irrational, and quite honestly,
ignorant to the way business works. There's a
reason contracts exist and if she wants to pretend
she got screwed then that's on her. I can explain
it to her, but I can't understand it for her.

*With a majority of her previously released music
re-recorded, this was her way of sticking it to
"the man" that would be Wayne Silverman.*

Martha Fox
Look, it isn't just about him. He made himself an
enemy. But this isn't about him.

Naomi Wilde
This is about a girl trying to be herself in a world
that wants to control her.

Hanna Chance
Tell you how to dress, how to look, how to be
sexier.

Ashton Craig
This is about her being a positive female role model
for young girls everywhere.

Martha Fox
This is about a young girl with a big dream making
a statement.

Naomi Wilde
This is about pushing back.

Hanna Chance
Speaking up.

Ashton Craig
Smiling in the face of your oppressor.

Martha Fox
Taking back control.

Hanna Chance
This is her story and she is only making sure it's
written and remembered the way she wants it to be.

Naomi Wilde
By the end, Phoebe will be undeniable. People don't
have to like her or her music, but they will have
to respect her body of work.

Ashton Craig
Numbers don't lie. By every metric she is demol-
ishing the music industry and paving a new way for
distribution. Labels used to take a lion's share on
the back end, but Phoebe has shown the world that
if you have a platform, it's yours to use however
you choose.

Martha Fox
At the end of the day, Phoebe wins. No more men
saying no. No more men gatekeeping. No more petty
obstacles.

Hanna Chance
She gets to continue doing what she loves and being
one hundred percent herself and I think that is
something special.

Phoebe Fox
I love all of you, more than you could ever know.
The 'Through the Years' world tour is happening and
I hope you all come out to a show. I would love
to see all of your beautiful faces in the crowd
while we sing together and be friends. I'll see you
there. [Phoebe winks at the camera.]

*With Phoebe Fox kicking off her much anticipated
'Through the Years' stadium tour, it remains to
be seen how her growth will be on display. There
aren't many acts on international stadium tours
and based on the explosion of support from a
passionate—arguably rabid—fan base it is a foregone
conclusion that this tour expects to be one of the
biggest events in pop culture history.*

*People can look back and say they were there, or
what they were doing when Phoebe Fox was in town.
Many around her stand to benefit greatly from her
business model and the independent machine that she
has built. Phoebe Fox is coming .□ □ □ □ □ and .the
world is waiting.*

[Phoebe Fox's music plays while statistics and
sales metrics appear up on the screen. Timelines
and graphs illustrate the clear decline in her old
recordings versus her new recordings. The credits
begin to roll as the documentary comes to an end.]

25

After landing at JFK and calling my mom again to arrange an Uber, I find myself standing outside of his building. Ashton's building.

I've been anxious about what I'm even going to say to him when I see him. Does he know I'm alive? Would anyone have tipped him off? I know a million things I want to say to him. I want to ask him how he could set me up, but mostly . . . why? I felt like we were building something strong and heading in a good direction.

He felt safe to me.

Comfortable.

His hug, warm like home.

That home is burnt to the ground now.

The building towers over me, like every building in the city. Tall structures create man-made valleys where the sun can only reach partially. I take my time building up the courage to walk into the lobby. The revolving door feels heavier than I remember on my way in, feeling it's weight resisting my push. The momentum eventually takes over and carries me through. It feels like the building is swallowing me whole and hard not to imagine as my heart sinks into the pit of my stomach. I feel it climb up my throat and try to will myself to keep pushing forward. It's time to close this chapter of my life and begin writing my next story.

A young woman sits behind a large desk, where she stands watching me approach with slow-paced steps.

"Good afternoon. Is there something I can help you with?"

"Um . . . yeah, hi. I'm here to see Ashton Craig."

"Sure. Would you like me to call him and let him know you're here?"

"I know where he . . . can I just go up?"

"Oh, yeah. Absolutely," she says to me with a smile that overtakes her face.

"Thank you so much," I tell her as I walk to the elevators. She sits back down and I press the *up* button to call the elevator, waiting patiently as I can hear the whirring sound of mechanical parts working just beyond the big metal doors. The motorized movement stops and a digital bell sounds as the doors spread apart, letting the artificial light flood out like a welcoming invitation to the rest of my life.

I step onto the elevator and press the button to take me to Ashton's floor. I look down at my clean hands as my fingers dance against my thighs. The last time I was on an elevator it was an ascension into uncertainty, but an escape from unspeakable horrors. The purple and red bruises on my wrists remind me of those horrors. I find silver linings knowing that this elevator ride isn't me fleeing my impending doom.

I'm let off and my feet carry me into a hallway with gray carpet and navy blue walls. Ashton's condo is at the far end of the hall. I've been here a handful of times now, luckily, otherwise I don't know that I'd get to have this intimate confrontation. The walk to his door seems long. There are only five other doors between the elevator and his but each door feels miles apart. Each step I take is a little heavier as I get closer. Those navy blue walls flash in my mind, becoming rocky, like the tunnel back at the Exhibit. The other doors flash, becoming deep and treacherous tunnels that go on until the darkness swallows the end of those halls. My head aches under the artificial light and the sinking weight in my belly begs me to turn back, but my heart burns for validation and the heart wants what the heart wants. I close my eyes and count to five, slowly and when I open them, it's all gone.

I stand right outside of his door, staring at the peephole, wondering how I'll look to him if he sees me. I wonder what his reaction might be with the door between us when he does. If he will even open it and acknowledge me. Maybe he'll play it cool. Maybe he will deny everything. My head is a whirlwind with thoughts and the longer I stand here the more my feet feel like they're taking root through the floor.

"Okay, Phoebe. You got this. Just breathe," I whisper to myself. I take several deep breaths and think I'm ready. "Okay."

Knock, knock, knock, knock, knock,

I tap fast and soft. Time creeps slowly as I wait eager and nervous, hoping I don't look as out of place as I feel in these clothes. I imagine him seeing me through the peephole and not answering so I cover it with my hand.

I bet he comments on my hat, knowing I'm not a baseball fan, or much of a sports fan at that. I hear footsteps coming from the other-side of the door and despite why I'm here, I involuntarily straighten myself up like this is a first date. I feel pathetic, but also angry that my body betrays me and responds this way. We didn't come here to be cute or look pretty.

The door opens and there he stands, eyes wide with shock. "Phoebe," he stands there, speechless. It's hard to peg what he's thinking but whatever it is, I get the sense he didn't expect me here. "Wh-where have . . ." I raise a single eyebrow at him as I watch his eyes learn my new bruises and see the echoes from the most terrifying experience of my life. He shuffles aside. "Please, come in, come in."

I hesitate for a moment, taking an extra beat to study him. His body language seems erratic. Is he truly surprised? . . . Embarrassed even? I step through the threshold as he closes the door behind me. I can't help but wonder what version of myself will emerge from this condo. We stand in his open kitchen where he frantically opens a cabinet and pulls out two glasses.

"I, uh, I wasn't expecting you here. Aren't you supposed to be in the Netherlands?" He reaches for a bottle of red wine on his counter.

"I don't want any, thank you. We need to talk."

"Yeah, yeah, yeah, totally," he says, pouring himself a glass. I watch him put the bottle back and I notice the knife block on the counter beside it. He waves me to follow him into the livingroom. A small sectional couch sits across from a large TV and a small computer desk. Living in New York means there is a value to minimalism, and despite the apartment being small, it's quite large compared to others like it. I follow him in. "Please, sit. Tell me, what's uh . . . what's up?"

Is he nervous? I think he's nervous. He is definitely off. I find it suspicious he wouldn't have heard about what happened. Is he playing dumb? If so, maybe I will play along—if only for a moment. I find it hard to believe that a professional journalist would have avoided hearing about me. Certainly mutual friends or others who know we're dating would have reached out. "So, you didn't hear what happened?

He takes a big pull from the glass, wiping his mouth with the back of his hand after a gasp. "No. Catch me up. I'm so happy to see you."

I feel myself watching him too closely. "Well, I just flew in after having a quite interesting forty-eight hours."

He sits the near empty glass down on the glass coffee table in front of us. His expression becomes serious in a way that is unfamiliar to me. I'm used to it being upbeat and playful, sweet and charming. This is new to me. "Did something happen? Are you alright?"

He's improvising. He hasn't even acknowledged how beat up and battered I look. What kind of boyfriend—nevermind, that's not why I'm here.

"Were you in a car wreck?" Nevermind, there it is. Ironic that he should ask that. "You look like you need a doctor, Pheebs. Would you like me to go with you I can-"

"Actually," I interrupt. "I was in a car accident, funny enough . . . but these aren't from that," I say, gesturing to my face. I roll up my sleeves to make sure he sees my wrists. The discoloration is even more dramatic to look at than it feels now. I see him look at them.

"Pheebs, uh . . ." he leans forward, lowering his voice, talking with a more measured tone. "We should really get you to a doctor."

"I'm fine!" I snap. "Listen, Ashton . . ." I watch him like a hawk. He is less rattled than before. He's adjusted and has had time to think. I don't know what he knows, but I don't know that I believe anything he will say at this point. "Are you telling me nobody has called, texted, emailed, nothing? Have you not watched the news yesterday or today?"

He grabs the glass again and leans back in his seat, throwing his leg across his other. "Phoebe, why don't you save the song and dance and just tell me what's really going on? You don't call, you just . . . show up in New York? Here?"

A grin creeps across my face and I can't help but chuckle. I'm shaking my head *no* at how unbelievable this man is acting right now. "Okay. So that's how we're going to play it? Alright, I'll play."

"Play what?" he asks, raising his voice. That's an octave I've never heard from him. "Who is playing? If anything I could ask you the same thing."

"Cut the shit, Ash. I know what you did." Fuck, I shouldn't have played that card yet. The heat in my face rises and my heart is dancing in my chest.

Ashton stares through me, his smoldering eyes ready for a fight. He plays with his tongue inside his mouth. "Okay . . . and why don't you enlighten me." He takes another drink from the glass, this time finishing it. He lets out a refreshing gasp. "What exactly do you know that I did?" He sits the now empty glass on the table and I can't help but notice a snowglobe he has on the table with New York City inside. I imagine it glowing from all of the lights and then wonder how heavy it would feel in my hand if I were to hold it.

"Scott told me everything." It's out now. I feel my throat swell and my muscles tensing. I hope it's not as obvious as I feel. I stare at the coffee table—more at the legal pad with writing scrawled on it. A cheap ink pen with no cap sitting beside it. A red three-wick candle that's been burned before. I'm going to guess it's apple pie or cinnamon.

"And what did New Guy tell you exactly?"

All of a sudden I find it annoying that Ashton is calling him New Guy, like he was part of the team. That nervous feeling is replaced by anger again as I stare at his face. He's just sitting there . . . smug and cocky like he knows why I'm here. Like he knows what I've come here to say. "Scott told me that you were the one who arranged for my team to be attacked."

"Attacked!? . . . Are you serious right now? Scott said that?" he asks with little bursts of laughter between his words. "Are you fucking with me? Tell me you're joking."

I burst from the couch to my feet. "Look at my fucking face Ashton," I shout down at him, pointing to the obvious marks. "Does it look like I'm fucking joking!?"

Ashton stands just as fast to meet my anger on his feet as he stands taller than me. "Don't you raise your voice at me like I'm some kind of child! Who the fuck do you think you are coming into my house and screaming–"

"I'm Phoebe fucking Fox and I know exactly who–" Ashton's hand grabs my entire face and I fall back into the couch, hard against his push. I feel every ache and pain in my body from before he shoved me as I try to get back to my feet.

"Ah, fuck, fuck, fuck!" he shouts as he comes over to try and help me up.

I jerk away from him. "Get the fuck off me!" I tell him as I get back to my feet without his help. "What the fuck are you doing, putting your hands on me!?"

"Phoebe, fuck. I'm so sorry. You know I didn't . . . I'm not that kind of guy, I just . . . you were screaming, talking down to me, I just . . . "

"It's over . . . we're done."

"Phoebe, listen–"

"No! You listen! You don't get to set me up and then pretend you didn't have anything to do with it."

"Phoebe, I'm telling you right now, I didn't set you up, we can call Scott right now and–"

"We can't call Scott!" I interrupt with a cackle as I begin to pace his living room floor.

"Why not? I have his number."

"First off, I think it's weird you would even have his number . . . and second, Scott is dead."

Ashton stares at me with the coffee table between us. "What the fuck are you talking about?"

"I know about The Exhibit or whatever they wanna call it."

"The Exhibit?"

I see we're back to playing stupid. "Yeah, you know, the dirty fucking warehouse where they auction off human beings to psychos to turn into their twisted little guinea pigs!? The one in the middle of nowhere with armed guards that looks like an art museum? That one!"

Ashton stands there silent, shaking his head as he stares at the floor. He looks up at me. "And you're telling me you were there and now you're here, and you killed Scott."

"How else would I get here?"

I can sense his vibe change entirely. He's pacing around the table and starting to feel more like a cornered raccoon. My gut is begging me to just run out the door and take the stairs, but I know if he wanted to he would catch me. I don't know that I'm in any condition to run now. "I don't know what happened, but you weren't supposed to leave there. Whatever you did though, you still managed to find your way back here and now it looks like I'm just another bitter ex, huh?" He picks up the wine glass and tosses it from hand to hand like a baseball. "And you thought what? You'd come here and tell me what for and that you were gonna turn me in? You gonna write a shitty song about me for little teen future sluts to dance to? How did you expect this to go?" He tosses the wine glass at me and I scream, ducking fast enough to barely avoid it as it shatters on the wall behind me. "Did you expect to just walk in here, rattle my cage and then just walk back out!?"

He walks toward me fast and before I can even think to run I stumble over my own feet and fall. He reaches down, grabbing my cardigan and pulling me up. I see his teeth gritting and smell the wine on his breath. I grab the largest piece of the wine glass off the floor as he pulls me up.

"There's only one way you're leaving here, bitch!"

As he threatens me I slam my hand with the jagged end of the shard as hard as I can into his face.

"Ahhh! Fucking hell!"

He drops me and I fall harder than when I fell on my own. I scramble back to my feet. I slice my palm in the process of holding the piece of sharp glass and ball my hands into fists to try and keep from bleeding. I feel my heartbeat in my hand.

I'm ready to fight and don't know what to expect from him. He stares at me seething as he slides the glass out of his face and drops it onto the floor.

"Oh, you fucked up now. You *really* fucked up!" The blood pours down his face as he staggers toward me. I back away, now in the kitchen and he is coming at me too fast to react. I scramble away over to the sink counter and grab a knife from the wooden block. I take another just for insurance, holding them out at him with the menace of the pointy end.

"Get the fuck back, Ashton. I am *not* playing around!"

"What are you gonna do, dear?" he snickers. "You gonna cut me?" he mocks, taking slower—more calculated—steps toward me. "You gonna stab me like I owe you money? Hmm?"

He knows he can't let me leave here and we both know it. He lunges at me and I jab at him with a knife and he swats my bruised wrist away, causing me to drop it. He grabs me by my throat and shoves me against the counter and instinctively I stab him in his shoulder with the other knife.

He doesn't even acknowledge it, slamming the back of my head against the counter harder, causing all of the air to leave my body while my head throbs. He twists my wrist and tosses me aside, back into the living room where I stumble on my feet like a sloppy drunk trying to dance. He pulls the knife out of his shoulder and tosses it into the sink. "You got me fucking good, Pheebs. You've got more fight in you than I would've guessed."

You have no idea.

I stand here just trying to catch my breath with his couch behind me and before I can find words to speak he kicks me in the chest so hard I tumble over it backward, slamming through the coffee table as it shatters to pieces.

"For fuck's sake, Phoebe, look at you. You broke my damn coffee table!" he says, in the most asshole of tone he can muster.

I lay here, wrapped in the metal frame, twisted legs, and shards of broken glass waiting for him to just put an end to it already. Fuck, that really hurt . . . and I'm tired of fighting. Sharp points kiss my skin as I move to sit up. Tinkling sounds from the glass falling as I try to move quickly, only to be slowed by the battered body I'm stuck with. Ashton steps over me and smiles. His hands reach down and grab for my throat as I try to fend him off. My grabbing and smacking is urgent but I'm exhausted. I can feel it in my attacks.

He drops to his knees despite the glass on his floor. His eyes bulge as his teeth are bared and clenched while he chokes the air out of me. I let my hands fall away from his immovable grip and I start feeling around above my head. I feel an ink pen I think. I don't take much time to figure it out, I just grab a hold tight and I stab him in the arm. It's three times before he lets my neck go and snatches the pen away. I try to roll onto my side in an attempt to crawl away, but he is on top of me and in control. I can't get away.

I'm trapped.

My arms are outstretched and ready to cling onto anything. I feel Ashton's hand on my shoulder, pulling me to lay on my back again, but as I feel him pulling me my fingers find his New York skyline snow globe among the destruction from the coffee table. As I get the smooth ball in my palm I am slung onto my back. Using the momentum I swing the snow globe and the jagged corner from the solid base bashes the side of his head causing him to topple over beside me. The trapped air escapes from my chest and I raise up and hit him again, this time harder in the same spot.

"Okay!" I hit him again. "Stop!" he shouts, begging with a sudden fragility in his voice. His hands shielding his head. His legs curling up with his body like a beaten child.

I don't stop though . . . I swing again, blood flinging away each time I raise the tall buildings of NYC in my hand.

Again! I hit him in the eye and can feel the hardness of the bone soften and crunch under the punishing blow.

I roar as I hit him again, and again, and again, until his fight stops and I stand atop him, staring down with my heart racing. Blood paints his living room in such an abstract way that I can't help but find beauty in it. Serenity . . . finality. Maybe I'm just as sick as him and this is my art. Maybe the difference between us is that I'm not seeking an exhibit to showcase it.

I stare down at my hand and the bloody snow globe and hold it up closer. The snow inside is chaotic within the held confined scale-sized city and it brings me a sense of peace. I feel a warm enveloping sense of accomplishment as I step away from Ashton's bloody self and head to his sink. I grab a glass from the cabinet and pour myself some red wine from a new bottle. This is to celebrate. I am Phoebe Fox and I am sick of people telling me I can't, telling me why I won't, and putting obstacles in my way. Here is to continuing to grow and move forward. I raise the glass to the living room as if there is an audience hearing me give the toast in my head. The show must go on.

ACKNOWLEDGEMENTS

This book wouldn't be what it is without the help and support from a list of people. Many of which I consider friends now. This started as an idea that I got way too excited about and then it just got way out of control, but these are all of the enablers who were responsible for making this all it could be.

Kaylynn, you always do a great job proofing and editing my scribbling (can I call it scribbling if I'm typing? What is a word for scribbling with the keyboard?) and I feel like our back and forth with each book leads me to learning something new that I carry into the next thing. I love you and I like you. Thanks for being a wonderful partner and my best friend and calling me out on my nonsense in each new manuscript (and enduring my rants about ideas that never catch any wind). I was excited to write this book and follow through with it because I knew you would appreciate a story about a pop star under duress. I hope I delivered on that for you.

Christy Aldridge, your patience and willingness to rise to the challenge of any idea I present to you is admirable. I appreciate you so much for what you do and how you deliver. I'm always pleased with how you give my stories a face. Presentation is everything and you're a huge role in that. Thank you for your work on the first edition cover.

A special shout out to Fabled Beast Design for the second edition cover.

Joey Powell, it's always a pleasure to partner with you. The interior of this book is what it is because of you and I won't stop demanding people to go to you for interior work as long as you're offering it. Thanks for always being clutch and willing to listen to ideas (even when they don't pan out.)

Amy Tackett, Danielle Morris, Mo Medusa, this book is a much lesser book without your contributions as alpha readers. You three helped call me on things early and ultimately helped sharpen just who Phoebe Fox is in this story. Thank you immensely for all of your help. The painful alpha reader phase was less painful with you three and I consider myself very fortunate to have had your help.

Charity Massengale, Karly Latham, thank you so much for being beta readers for this story. I know early on I talked about this story to you both and I think your excitement only made me want to rope you into the process even more.

All of the authors who answered the call when I asked for blurbs, a huge thank you! I greatly appreciate the time commitment to react to this story. (Everyone is mentioned in the front of the book, on the praise page where my ego can be seen blushing and breakdancing.)

Advance Readers, people on social media who helped talk about and share this book and really build up excitement. Thank you to all of you!

And you, for taking a chance on this book. Whether it was for the cover, or the synopsis, or a friend told you, or you let me sucker you into reading words I wrote, thank you, thank you, THANK YOU!

Sunday afternoon, Phoebe Fox was admitted to a medical facility where she received treatment for a severe onset illness. After careful consideration it has been decided with a heavy heart that The Through Years Stadium Tour will have to postpone the upcoming shows for The Netherlands and Switzerland dates.

Due to these unforeseen circumstances, fans will have the option to be refunded. We understand how unfortunate it may be to anyone traveling who may have booked travel and lodging. We're unable to accommodate those expenses. In the meantime the team will be working hard to reschedule the affected dates and anyone who chooses not to be refunded may keep the tickets which will be accepted/scanned upon entry at the rescheduled dates. More information to come as soon as it is available.

We sincerely want to extend our deepest apologies to the fans. Phoebe and the entire team take immense pride in being dependable night in and night out for all you and Phoebe is committed to making this right.

In the meantime, we ask that at this time that everyone respect Phoebe's privacy. She will recover as quickly as she can and be back better than ever.

@**moon__chick983**: So grateful she's safe and sound! 

@**rebel__in__love222**: I heard she was getting a facelift

@**d3ath__m3tal.92**: So I guess she didn't get kidnapped? 🌫️ bummer

@**bl00dandb0nez**: I don't even believe this. Probably just a publicity stunt.

@**foxluvr99**: So happy to hear she's okay!

@**bitchy.witch00**: wait... wut happened? She cancelled a series of multimillion dollar shows because she is a little tired? Why does everyone love her so much again?

@**foxy.lady10812**: I don't know whether to be upset that I have to wait for the rescheduled show or be happy that she's okay! 

@**the__amy__t__95**: Praying for Phoebe Fox and her recovery 🖤

ABOUT THE AUTHOR

David lives in the Greater Cincinnati area (in Northern Kentucky for any locals who choose to argue about geography) where he lives with his two teen sons and the lady of the house. When David isn't fighting imposter syndrome as a writer he is probably working out, watching horror movies, baseball, or wrestling.

Suspense and tension are David's playground and he has independently self-published multiple books in addition to having short stories published in several anthologies.

Other Works

Short Horror

The Tickle Monster

Kill ~~the bugs~~ For Me